Talk to Me

D. K. SUTTON

Cover Designer: Amy Queau Q Design

Editor: Lia Fairchild Finishing Touch Editing

Created with Vellum

Acknowledgments

My family for supporting me all the times I'm off writing or editing or some other writing related activity. Tristan and Shayna for sharing their experiences on working as tech support for a media company. Ryan and Tristan for helping me with my website.

My writing group, R&M, for always being supportive. Abby for guiding and not getting frustrated by my questions.

My sisters for providing feedback on Talk to Me and always supporting me. A special thank you to my sister Kelly who has been a part of this journey with me since I started writing fifteen years ago. She's part editor, part cheerleader, and always by my side when I need her.

My fellow authors for the invaluable information and support you provide me.

ONE
Max

"I DON'T THINK HE KNOWS WHO YOU ARE." Dylan threw the line out innocently as if he didn't know it would rile me up.

"Are you kidding me?" I relaxed my hand before my lunch, a tasty PB&J sandwich, died a mangled death. I placed it on the lunch table, mostly intact, and turned to my friend. We'd known each other since high school, and for the last two years, we'd worked together at Coxx Communications as customer service reps. I loved working with my best friend, but today he was testing the limits of our friendship. I rolled my neck, easing the tension that had been building all day. It started when they released the performance numbers. "I'm the guy who's right behind him in customer satisfaction. He knows who I am." The company released everyone's numbers to spark competition and gave bonuses to the best. I used to be on top, but that was before Chase Corrigan started six months ago.

"No one remembers the guy in second."

"Ouch." I put my hand over my heart, pretending to search for bullet holes.

"I'm just saying. You're one of a hundred employees. This competition—this tension between you—is all in your head."

"I disagree. He may not like me, and I mean at all, but I guarantee you he knows who I am. Yesterday, he glared at me for just being in the same room."

Dylan smiled, exposing the dimples in his cheeks. He exuded boy-next-door charm by the bucketful. I was immune to his charms, thankfully. He was straight and in a relationship with a girl who could kick my ass. "Dude, you are not special. He treats everyone like that."

Was I overreacting? I thought back to the moment yesterday in the copy room. Jon had been waiting in line as I stood by the door. Chase finished making copies and walked by him, ignoring him as if Jon was an ant beneath his notice. He glanced up at me right before walking out the door. The glare he'd given me could have melted metal with its intensity. I shook my head at the memory. "No way. You're wrong."

Dylan smirked, crossing his arms as he stared out at something behind me. I recognized the scheming glint in his eyes.

"What?"

"Time to put up or shut up," he said.

"That's not how you use that phrase."

"Your money dumbass. Five dollars says your boy hates everyone—heck anyone—as much as you."

"How?"

"Have someone talk to him. If he snaps at them, it shows you're not special."

I hesitated but only for a second. Chase's frosty attitude toward me when we happened to be at the elevators at the same time in the mornings infuriated me and did not excite me at all. Sure, Chase wore the hell out of his tight chinos and his bright button-down shirts that clung to his slim muscular body, but that didn't mean he could treat people the way he did. Treat me the way he did. People loved me; I was a people person. It was obvious that Chase Corrigan was not. He treated others as if they were beneath his notice, but he reserved his hostility for me. This was a sucker bet. "Make it ten and loser has to watch any video the winner chooses."

"I told you, I'm not watching those stupid killer cat videos."

"Scared I'll win?"

"Not at all," Dylan said as glanced at Chase, took a deep breath, and stood up.

I grabbed his arm and pulled him back down. "What are you doing?" I glanced around making sure no one noticed us. "It can't be you. Who knows what you'll say to him."

"Whatever. Come with me. You can listen in."

"My being there taints the whole thing." I shook my head. We'd done hundreds of these experiments over the years. Some called them pranks, but really, they were just ways to establish bragging rights. Dylan knew the rules. "We need someone impartial."

We surveyed the room. Most everyone had gone back to work. It wasn't long before I found the perfect person. "How about James?" Everyone loved him. He didn't have a mean bone in his body.

"You're kidding."

"You did say anyone."

"Fine." Dylan shrugged and called him over.

"What's up, guys?"

"We want you to talk to Chase. Just say hi."

He furrowed his brow. "Why?"

"Just to be friendly—" Dylan started.

"We made a bet," I interrupted. It wasn't like our antics weren't legendary. Honesty was the best course of action at this point.

James shook his head. "You guys never quit," he said. Still, he hesitated as he glanced over at our target. I didn't blame him. Chase could be scary as hell. "Okay," he said finally. "I'm in. But not because I agree with what you're doing. I just think that guy could use a friend."

"Good enough."

James slowly approached Chase, glancing back at us for encouragement. Dylan waved him on. Chase stood next to the microwave, heating his lunch.

I held my breath, wondering what Chase would do. Surely he wouldn't snap at James, but I couldn't be positive. He didn't seem to like anyone.

As James reached him, Chase turned around, his expression wary. James kept his distance as he talked to him. No one was crazy enough to touch him. The bubble around Chase might as well have been a brick wall. We couldn't hear the words James said, but we could see Chase's reaction. His jaw clenched and his arms crossed protectively as he glared at James. He said something, and James's hands went up defensively.

"Heck and heck yeah," Dylan said. "I win." My friend was on a no swearing kick courtesy of his girlfriend, so his cuss words were suitably inventive.

"That's not a saying."

"Don't be a sore loser."

I reached for my wallet about to admit defeat, when Chase glanced past James, scanning the room. When his eyes reached mine, he glared, grabbed his food, and stomped off.

"Don't use me in any more of your 'experiments,'" James said when he reached us.

"What did you say?" Dylan asked.

"Did you mention me?"

"What? No. I said hi. How are you today? That's it."

Dylan shook his head, pulling two fives from his wallet and slamming them on the table. "You win, dude. That guy despises you."

As I pocketed the money, I didn't feel like I'd won anything. Chase definitely noticed me, and assumed I'd put James up to harassing him. And of course, I had. But my unease wasn't just because there was someone out there who hated me that much. Chase assumed someone saying hi to him must be a trick. What a sad and lonely life. The guy brought it on himself, of course, but it still bothered me. I shook those thoughts away. Karma was a bitch and so was Chase Corrigan most of the time. I wasn't going to lose any sleep over it.

The last caller before my break had been an asshat. He complained about everything. Then he asked me where I was from as if he was questioning my intelligence. When I told him Missouri, trying to be friendly and provide good customer service, the guy said, "Do you think I really care?" I politely put him on hold for a second, before I did something I'd regret, like telling him off. Although I'd fixed his problem, the call wouldn't help my customer service numbers.

After the call, I engaged my BRB (Be Right Back) to take a short break. I started to say something to Dylan but stopped. Chase stood by my desk, regarding me coolly with icicle blue eyes. His long blond hair, which I was not obsessed with, framed his delicate face. God, he was fucking gorgeous. Especially when his eyes sparked with anger. He slammed a paper on my desk and walked away. His fury seemed to put an extra sway in his ass. I watched until Chase turned the corner.

Dylan rolled his chair over. "What was that?"

"I don't know." I stared at the last spot I'd seen him in.

Fingers snapped in front of my eyes, and I glanced back at my friend. Dylan pointed down at the paper on my desk. "This might be a clue."

I flushed, ignoring his knowing look. "Right."

I picked up the note and read it.

Maxwell, please leave me the fuck alone.

I handed the note to Dylan. "He definitely knows who I

am." I really shouldn't be so happy about that, but it wasn't the only thing making me smile. Perfect Chase no-single-hair-would-dare-be-out-of-place Corrigan. The note somehow made him seem more human.

"Why are you grinning like an idiot?" Dylan asked.

I pointed at the note. "Chase Corrigan has terrible handwriting."

TWO
Chase

I IGNORED THE STARES FROM MY COWORKERS as I made my way to the staff lounge. The only thing on my mind was coffee. And hoping I didn't run into Maxwell Sloan. Was it too much to ask to just be left alone?

I loved my job. I really did. I just preferred interacting with others in small doses or over the phone. Maxwell's stunt yesterday brought back all the scrutiny I never wanted and had hoped to avoid. This job could get monotonous, so I understood people wanted something to talk about. I just wanted it to be someone else. Anyone else.

Thankfully, the lounge was empty. I always arrived early so I'd have time for a cup of coffee before my first call. Today, Amica had stopped me in the hall, and that set me back a few minutes. She was a sweet girl and if I wanted to be around others, she would be one of my favorites. But at this moment, coffee was all I could think about.

The lounge walls had attempted to be cheery with yellow paint but faded into failure. The single-cup coffee maker sat waiting to disburse its goodness, beckoning to me. That first cup was the only thing on my mind. The office coffee committee had some generic stuff, but I brought my own K-cups. I was particular about things. Nothing wrong with that except it reinforced others' opinions that I was peculiar. Difficult. Stuck up. I'd heard the whispers, some said so loud they barely qualified as such, but I didn't care. I came to Coxx Communications to work. I wasn't here to make friends. Not that I'd ever been particularly good at that anyway.

I was used to the frosty atmosphere in the office. It wasn't just because I didn't socialize with everyone and spent my breaks chatting about the weekend and who slept with who. No, part of the resentment came from my customer rep numbers. As soon as I started, I was able to rise to the top, beating out Maxwell. I had to admit, I enjoyed knocking him out of first. I didn't care about being in first place. Not really, but people like Maxwell Sloan drove me crazy. They were loud, obnoxious, and thought they could charm the world. I wouldn't fall for that act. I'd learned my lesson.

Everyone assumed I wasn't good with people. That I had no social skills. And they couldn't figure out how I could do my job so well. I could talk to people over the phone easier than in person. I think it had to do with control. If I needed to, I could end the interaction with the push of a button. Not so easy to do in person. Also one-on-one wasn't as much of an issue. Groups really bothered me. I hated everyone watching me. Waiting for me to fail.

I did my job, and I was proud of how well I was doing. And if it bothered Maxwell that I beat his numbers every month, that was just the cherry on top.

The first time I met Maxwell Sloan, he hit on me, thinking I was a girl. I still remember the look in his eyes when he realized I wasn't. He stammered and backed away as if I could infect him with my gayness. It was the only time I'd ever seen him flustered.

I'd been mistaken for a woman before. That was the risk

you took when you wore your hair long, and I wasn't a beefy guy. I had a slim body. Still, I didn't care what people thought about my hair or my sexual orientation.

The coffee only took moments to brew but it felt like hours. I wanted to get it and go before anyone else tried to talk to me. Just thinking about yesterday pissed me off. I couldn't believe James had been a part of Maxwell's joke.

"Thinking about me?"

I turned around, my heart pounding at the sound of his voice. How had Maxwell known I was thinking about him? He watched me closely, his intense blue eyes contrasting with the humor in his voice and the charming smile on his face. My mouth had dropped open in surprise and I snapped it shut.

Max nodded at my hand, which had been gripping my spoon so tightly my knuckles were white. "I get that reaction all the time."

I kept myself from snorting at that remark as I dropped the spoon. "Go away." Trying to not let his closeness affect me, I removed my cup of creamy hazelnut coffee from the coffee machine. I still hadn't had that essential first drink, and I needed all the help I could get when dealing with Maxwell. He was arrogant and way too good-looking. I could tell he went to the gym; he had the muscles to prove it. But no matter how attractive he was and how well he fit into his dress pants, I couldn't get past his obnoxious personality. I reached for the sugar. Hopefully, ignoring him would achieve what my words had not.

"I just wanted to apologize for yesterday."

"Which part?" I turned to face him, tired of his crap. "The part where you tried to humiliate me or the part where you did it in front of everyone?"

"That wasn't my intention," he said, looking down. "I was just making a point."

"And what point was that?"

His mouth opened and then shut. He shook his head, avoiding my gaze.

I willed away the tears that threatened. He didn't need to say it. I knew the point. *Let's watch Chase Corrigan fall apart because he's socially inept.* I let my hair fall forward to cover my face as I scooped sugar onto my spoon. I couldn't bear for him to see the pain I felt at his words. I'd survive. I'd been here before.

Resolved, I reached for my coffee. Only, it wasn't there.

Maxwell sipped from my Yoda cup, smacking his lips. "What kind is this?" he asked. "I like it."

I stared at him in horror. I couldn't believe he drank my coffee.

"What? It was only a little sip."

But I couldn't talk. Adrenaline raced through me as I tried to push away my rage. I didn't drink after anyone. Ever. It was disgusting. My break was almost over, and I didn't have time to make another cup. I wanted to throttle him. I stretched my fingers out, trying to calm down, but it was no use. I hated him. I jabbed the spoon into the sugar bowl, wishing it was a knife I could stab him with. I wasn't usually violent, but Maxwell brought out the worst in me. I didn't say anything to him as I stormed from the room before I gave in to my murderous rage.

"Hey, Chase," Max said, his voice reaching me in the hallway. "Mind if I drink the rest of this?"

Bastard.

THREE

Max

THE CLOCK ON MY DESK TICKED DOWN to the start of the workday. The calls would soon pour in nonstop. I sipped Chase's coffee, enjoying the sweet drink. I added a ton of sugar. Guilt tugged at me, but it wasn't like he was going to drink it. No sense in wasting good coffee. I sighed when I thought of Chase.

The pain on his face when I tried to apologize bothered me. I honestly had expected him to ignore me. It wasn't like I could explain. I wanted to see if you hate me more than everyone else here. It was pathetic.

I tried to distract him with the coffee. He might have been a little angrier than I'd expected. Who knew the guy was a germophobe? I rubbed the back of my neck. I needed to forget about Chase and focus on work.

"If you want it, go get it," Dylan huffed out, nodding his head toward the east side of the building. He pulled his chair closer to my desk so we could talk without the rest of the office interceding. Not that they cared really. It was like working with a bunch of drones.

"It's not that easy," I said with a sigh. We stared across the room toward the target of our conversation. Cubicles as far as the eye could see obstructed our view. This would be a soul-sucking job if I didn't love certain aspects of it. Having my best friend for ten years beside me was definitely one of the perks.

"Man up, dude. I'm tired of listening to you whine about it."

Except when he was being a little bitch. "I've got this." But I didn't and we both knew it.

"Maybe you should just sleep with him already and get it over with."

"Please. He is not my type." I'm not sure how I said that with a straight face. I might not like Chase Corrigan, but he was every gay man's wet dream. Slim, firm build and a hot ass. His gorgeous face was all angles with intelligent pale blue eyes. Top that off with a long mane of light blond hair you could wrap your hands around... I pushed those thoughts away. Especially since Dylan was watching me with knowing eyes.

"Yeah, right," he said with a smirk. "Totally not your type."

"All I'm interested in is being the top customer service rep, and he's in my way."

"Maybe you shouldn't bitch-out the customers."

"That was one time. And that guy deserved it. Seriously, the problem was with his computer and not our equipment, and he still insisted I send out a tech. I just told him, politely I might add, that I'd send one out, but there was no way the tech could fix it because we weren't the problem."

"Why are you so competitive?"

"I'm not." At his raised eyebrow, I added, "I just like to win." When you had five siblings, everything was a competition. I shook my head. "I don't know how Chase does it. He bitches at everyone—"

"Not everyone. I think we've established it's mostly you."

I ignored that remark. "He's not friendly. He doesn't join in. He stays strictly in his lane and doesn't play well with others."

"I think you're pissed because there's someone out there immune to the Maxwell Sloan charm." Dylan grinned, enjoying this more than he should.

But he wasn't entirely wrong. Chase and I got off to a bad start. The first time we met, I hit on him. All that glorious long hair distracted me. The second he turned around all fire and fury, I knew it would never happen. I liked to have a good time. But Chase carried a seriousness about him, something that screamed—he didn't do casual. Unfortunately, or fortunately, however you wanted to look at it, casual was my go-to thing. I thought of the guy from Saturday night. What was his name again? Lucas? Levi? No, that wasn't right. Anyway, I had no desire to settle down. And although the challenge of something out of my reach was tempting, I liked my guys a little more thawed out. From that moment on, all I ever got from him was frosty looks, like I wasn't good enough to shine his stylish black boots.

Whatever. That was fine with me. I liked being on top. As in top customer service rep, not the sexual position. I liked to take more than give. The image of Chase pounding into me as his long hair teased the skin on my back arose unbidden. I pushed it out of my mind.

Chase Corrigan was in my way, and I needed to focus on that. I reminded Dylan of this. "It's about the money." There was a bonus involved and getting it was forever on the top of my to-do list.

"How does he get top rep?" he asked, shaking his head. "Every month."

"I don't know but it's pissing me off."

"That's what I'm talking about, Max. If you want it, go get it."

"How?" I had tried for months. Nothing I did seemed to matter. Customers loved Chase, and I just didn't fucking get it.

"I've got an idea." Dylan smiled deviously as he glanced around the room, making sure no one was listening. All of them were at their desks, working like the little drones they were. Hive mentality made a lot more sense to me since I started here.

"Go on. You have my attention," I said, lowering my voice even more.

"It involves bending the rules of the company and of decency," he added.

"Really? And you think I can beat him?"

"And bring him down a peg or two."

A flash of icicle blue eyes threatened my resolve. But then I remembered all the times Chase had treated me like an infectious disease he was afraid of catching.

"Fuck it," I said. "Whatever it is, I'm in."

FOUR

Chase

"IF YOU WANT YOUR INTERNET TO WORK, keeping your modem plugged in might help." I shut my eyes and took a deep breath. Normally, I was very professional. Number one in customer service satisfaction every month for the last six months. Part of that was because I was able to shut off my emotions and just focus on my work. At the moment, I was finding it very difficult. I pushed away thoughts of Maxwell Sloan, instead focusing on the call. "Yes, ma'am," I said, forcing a smile in my voice. "It happens all the time. You're welcome. And after the call, there will be a short survey. You can rate the service you got today at Coxx Communications."

I ended the call with a sigh, hoping I would have a few minutes before the next call came through. It wasn't the busiest time of day, so it was a possibility. I'd already used my BRB to grab another cup of coffee. I had to use a random cup from the cabinet. Just thinking about Maxwell drinking my coffee from my Yoda cup set my teeth on edge. There weren't enough words in the world to describe how much I detested Maxwell Sloan.

I felt bad for how I treated James yesterday. He was a genuinely nice guy, but I'd known as soon as I'd looked into those laughing eyes that Maxwell had been behind it. Why did I let him get under my skin? He was arrogant and thought everyone should love him. Everyone should be charmed by his all-American good looks and hot body. I could admit he had a hot body.

But if I was being honest with myself, I knew the reason Maxwell bothered me so much. But I wasn't going to think about Cameron. It was in the past.

This was not helping me get back on track. I took a deep breath, trying to find my peaceful center. Men like Maxwell and Cameron were all the same. I wasn't going to let them bother me. Or ruin my life any more than they already had.

I'd delivered my note to Maxwell, hoping that would be the end of it. Obviously, it hadn't worked. Maybe he really was trying to apologize. But I brushed away those thoughts. Maxwell didn't care about anyone but himself. Could I have used stronger language in my note? Or I could have told him instead of sending a note like a middle schooler. I really wasn't antisocial like everyone said. I hated the agony of small talk. I limited my interactions with people to those who really mattered. The only way to make it through the day successfully, calmly, was to limit the amount of energy taken away, like a battery. Interacting used up my energy. I was drained by the end of the day.

The strange thing was that interacting with Maxwell seemed to give me energy. It was mostly anger and frustration, but it was as if I'd been awakened from a deep sleep. I wasn't comfortable at all with it. I chalked it up to the fight-flight-freeze survival response. Usually I tended to go the flight or freeze route, but Maxwell brought out the fight in me. Where had it been hiding all this time? Where had it been hiding with Cameron?

This wasn't helping. Why did my thoughts always return to Maxwell? I straightened the picture of my sister, her husband, and their two little girls. The picture always seemed to help ground me. My sister, Sunny, and I were twins, but we looked nothing alike. There were similarities, like the blond hair, but her hair was short and sassy, just like her. The picture was calming, reminding me there were people in the world who loved me. People who accepted me. It was enough to calm me so when the next call came through, I was ready for it.

The last few hours of the afternoon slowed to a snail's pace. It gave me way too much time to think. So, I was relieved when another call came in.

"Hi, my name is Chase from Coxx Communications. How can I help you today?"

The line was quiet, and I worried the call had been dropped. The button was still lit, so I wasn't sure what was going on. "Hello, can I help you?"

"Yeah, sorry." The voice on the line was deep and somehow familiar. I shrugged off the feeling. I talked to hundreds of people a month. Of course, the voices would start to sound familiar. "I'm having some trouble," he continued. "Nothing seems to be working."

"Well then you've come to the right place. Can I have your name?"

"Mmm... How...Howard Hernandez."

This guy was definitely having problems, and it wasn't just with his Internet. He seemed to have problems with his own name. I wondered if he had some mental issues as well. Or maybe he was just shy. "Can I have your account number?"

"Okay." The voice sounded relieved. He rattled off his number without any hesitation.

I pulled up the account, noticing he lived on Hudson Street. I had a thing for alliteration. I loved names that began with the same letter. I almost had it with Chase Corrigan, but the difference in the sounds ruined it. This guy had his first and last name and street all start with H. People might think I was crazy for noticing things like that, but this job could be mind-numbing at times. Any distraction helped. Well, except for a certain arrogant jerk. I shook those thoughts off.

The account did belong to Howard Hernandez, and for some reason that surprised me. The guy seemed so unsure. But I got weird calls all the time, and this was probably going to be another one. "Well, everything looks fine on your account, Howard," I said. "What seems to be the problem?"

"My Internet isn't working. I mean I can't get it to work."

"I can help with that." I glanced at the basic list of things to do when the Internet wasn't working. They gave us cheat sheets. Not that I really needed them, but I wanted to go by the book. Supervisors reviewed calls and sometimes jumped on in the middle of the conversation. I had Howard turn the modem off, wait ten seconds, and turn it on again. "How about now?"

"No, still not working." Howard lost his stutter, seeming more confident.

"Is your phone connected to your Wi-Fi?"

"Yes."

"Is that working?"

"Yes, it is," he said, sounding surprised, but for some reason I didn't quite buy it. Something was off. I couldn't put my finger on it, though.

"Okay, let's look at your computer. Do you know how to find the Wi-Fi?"

"Yes."

"What does it say when you click on it?"

"No networks available."

"Okay, let's turn your computer off and on again to see if it will pick it up."

I waited while he did that. Then his deep voice once again came over the phone. "Okay, it's coming back on."

He had such a nice voice. I could almost get lost in the deep tones. I willed those thoughts away. "Can you see your Wi-Fi now?"

"No. Still not there."

If the phone worked, the problem had to be with his laptop. "Is your Wi-Fi enabled?" I asked. "Check your settings."

The sound of clicking reached me as he did what I asked. Then he let out a nervous laugh. "I'm so embarrassed," he said. "It's on airplane mode."

"Well, unless you're on a plane right now, I don't think you need that."

He laughed again, and it sounded more genuine than anything he'd said so far. My body reacted to the rich tone. The sound was so intimate it made me catch my breath. Do not get a hard-on while talking to a customer. But my body didn't listen.

"Anything else I could help you with?" I didn't want to end the call. I could have listened to his voice all day.

"I do have a question, if you don't mind."

"Of course."

"Where are you from?"

I hesitated. I sometimes got this question, but this was the first time I thought the person really wanted to know the answer. The calls were recorded, but I didn't want to seem rude. "Missouri, right now."

"But originally?"

"San Diego."

"I thought I detected a west coast vibe," he said warmly. "How long have you been in Missouri?"

I glanced at the clock. The call had gone over the strongly recommended fifteen-minute time frame. "A few years," I said vaguely. "Is there anything else I can assist you with?"

"No, I'm good." He hesitated for a beat. Was he trying to think of more questions just to keep me on the line.? That seemed crazy. "Thank you so much, Chase," Howard finally said. "Seriously, you've been very helpful."

"You're welcome." I explained the survey to him and let him know to call back if he had any additional problems.

It wasn't until after he'd hung up that I realized why the call had seemed so odd. The guy sounded young, despite his name, but he didn't seem to know much about electronics. That was unusual.

I'd gone well past the professional boundaries with the call, although I hadn't technically done anything wrong. I felt a connection with the caller. That had never happened to me before.

I pushed those thoughts to the back of my mind as another call came through. This one didn't go as well. I wasn't able to help the customer. She called about her cable not working and unfortunately, it was an outage problem. I tried to be polite, but she was insistent I should be able to fix it. I probably did not get a good customer review from her.

Later that afternoon, during my last break, I realized I hadn't thought about Maxwell much at all that afternoon. There were several hours when I didn't focus on him. At least that was something.

FIVE

Max

THE LAST PIECE OF PIZZA CALLED TO ME. I resisted the temptation. As the host, I needed to make sure that no one else wanted it. We probably should've ordered three pizzas instead of two.

"What did you say to your brother-in-law to get him to let you use his information?"

I shrugged as I reached for the piece of pizza. It had sat there for five minutes. It was fair game now, right? Besides, if we were going to talk about this, I needed the distraction.

"I told him it was a prank. We're known for our pranks, right?"

"You told him it was a prank?" Sadie leaned over Dylan so she could fix her stare on me. We were all squeezed together on the couch, playing video games. She was Dylan's girlfriend and they often came over together to play. I didn't mind at all. In fact, Sadie was a much better player than Dylan. Not that I would admit that to my friend. No way. The only issue was that sometimes watching them together brought up feelings of loneliness. It would be nice to have someone of my own to laugh with, play games with, and do stuff with. Of course, having regular sex would be nice too. I hooked up now and then but that sometimes got old.

"A prank," she repeated. "Is that really what you told him?"

"What was I gonna tell him?"

"The truth?" said Dylan.

"Really? So, I should have told him I was pretending to be a caller so I could find a way to beat this guy? You think that makes me look like a better person?"

"They're both pretty bad," Sadie said. "Not gonna lie."

"Thanks for that."

"What went wrong?"

I glanced at her in surprise. "What do you mean?"

Dylan answered instead. "Dude, your trash-talking is seriously lacking tonight. Something's going on."

I had my pizza in one hand and the controller in the other. I set the pizza back on the cardboard box and leaned back with a sigh. "I don't know. Chase on the phone talking to a customer is nothing like the Chase in the office. He was funny, charming, interesting..."

"You're crushing on him." Sadie had a knowing look on her face.

"No." I shook my head, but she only smiled. "I'm only interested in how to beat him," I said, maybe a bit too defensively, as I pretended to focus on the game.

"Dylan says he's hot."

I lost all pretenses at that, turning to my friend in surprise. "Really?"

"I did not," Dylan sputtered, then turned to Sadie. "I said Max thinks he's hot."

"Whatever. The way you described him sounded hot. What about it, Max? Is he hot or not?"

There was no point in denying it. I didn't think I could and sound credible. "Definitely hot," I said. "But it's like he's two different people. Which one is the real Chase? The smooth guy or the ice princess?"

"Is now the time to remind you that you were using a fake persona?"

"Touché."

"Don't you have a 'phone voice'?"

"But that's the point. When I'm talking to a customer, that's not the real me. I mean, not really. I don't know those people on the phone. He seems more real with customers than with his co-workers. That doesn't make sense."

"Maybe that's his secret. He's able to seem sincere with the customers." Dylan scratched Toby's head. When they'd first arrived, Toby barked at them like he'd never met them before, and now he was curled up in Dylan's lap. Traitor.

"Doesn't mean it's the real him."

"So what? You're trying to beat him, not date him."

I was so done with this conversation. I wanted to understand Chase Corrigan. It didn't mean I was interested in him. "Can we just play video games?"

Dylan and Sadie exchanged looks. I ignored them, preferring to demolish them at Gears of War instead.

"Cleaning up shit from Gonzo's cage," Carlos said. Gonzo was the gorilla at the local zoo. We were gathered around the conference room table, waiting for the team meeting to start.

"Cutting the grass at the golf course with only a pair scissors." Dylan raised his eyebrows in challenge. "What about you, Max?" he asked. "What would you rather be doing than sitting in this 'hecking' meeting?"

Everyone hated these meetings, even the bosses. They teamed up normally and had them together. I liked my supervisor, Sean. He was a cool guy. But the meetings were torture.

They went over a list during the meeting of everything you could possibly do wrong. And if they were talking about it, then some dumbass had done it. Boring regulations and office protocol also made it onto the agenda every time. A new thing they started, maybe to boost morale, was talking about new initiatives they wanted to start. No one else shared their enthusiasm. It was mind-numbingly boring.

I was about to answer Dylan when I noticed Chase pulling up a chair on the other side of the table. I didn't even realize Ben, the other supervisor hosting the meeting, was his supervisor.

"I'm exactly where I want to be," I said, smiling at them both.

Carlos gaped at me. "Who are you?"

"Yeah, dude," Dylan said, "You hate these things." As he turned toward me, he noticed Chase. "Oh. Never mind."

"What?" Carlos looked at Dylan and then back at me.

I kicked Dylan under the table. I didn't need everyone to know about my slight obsession with Chase. Thankfully, the supervisors walked in and saved me from having to explain.

At least now I had a diversion. I watched Chase closely, trying to figure out what made him tick. That was when I noticed it. He didn't have a single hair out of place, but he tapped his fingers on the table as if he were trying to dispel his nervous energy, a way to keep control. A bland smile appeared on his face as he kept his attention on the people talking in the front of the room. His back was ramrod straight. Was he resisting the urge to look my way?

"Anyone? What about you, Max?"

I tore my eyes away from Chase and looked up at my supervisor. Busted for not listening. I didn't even realize the meeting had started.

"Can you repeat the question?" I asked. No one was going to ruffle me today.

"We," he said, indicating the rest of the room, "were talking about the increasing turnover rates of our new employees. We wanted to give you guys a chance to weigh in on that. Any thoughts?"

I ignored the snickering from my friends and allowed myself a quick glance at Chase. He watched me with narrowed eyes. I winked at him, just to see the flush of red on his skin. Was that from anger, humiliation, or some other emotion? I'd love to find out but right now, I needed to come up with an answer. I didn't want Sean to move on. I liked having Chase's attention on me. I tapped my fingers against my chin as if I was thinking.

"New employees get plenty of training," I said finally, just before my supervisor gave up on me. He shook his head and was about to go on when I spoke. "And the supervisors are on the calls with them initially, but maybe we could do a buddy system." The guys beside me laughed and Chase turned away, shaking his head slightly, almost against his will.

"Like mentoring?" Ben stepped closer to me.

"Yes, exactly," I said, gaining momentum. What had started out as a way to gain attention from Chase and appease my sup, now seemed like a great idea. "The sups would have more time to do sup stuff, and the worker would have someone to go to if they needed a little help."

"Are you volunteering for this, Max?"

"Sure." I shrugged.

The guys laughed even harder. Okay so I wasn't always a good example for other workers to follow. But I did get the job done. And I'd had the highest numbers before Chase came along.

"Guys, can we take this seriously?" Sean gave them the death glare. He had used that look on me before. It was very effective. The guys shut up immediately. Ben cleared his throat, looking a little uncomfortable.

"I'd love to help," I continued. "And since we need the best of the best, maybe Chase would be interested.

There were a few overly dramatic gasps in the room.

"Oh, no you didn't," Dylan mumbled.

All eyes turned to Chase, and I immediately realized my mistake. I thought partnering with Chase would be a good way to get to know him better. Know thy enemy and all that. Instead, it focused everyone's attention on him. I could see him withdrawing more within himself. The change was minute. He always looked calm, cool, and collected on the outside. But his fingers curled together on the table.

"Chase? Is this something you might be interested in?" Ben walked over to him, talking to him as if he were the only one in the room.

"Of course," he said, his jaw firm. His eyes were the only thing about him that held any expression. And they were on fire.

"I love this idea, Max," Sean said. "We need a few more people. Any volunteers?" A few hands went up, but I wasn't paying attention, wondering if this was the best idea ever or the worst. I couldn't tear my eyes away from Chase. He stared ahead like he was afraid of losing his shit. At one point, he glanced at me and caught me staring. His look was a mixture of confusion, wariness, and a hint of murder.

"Thank you, guys. Please stay after the meeting so we can set up a time for the team to meet."

Dylan slapped me on the back, and I could tell without looking that he was grinning from ear to ear. Asshole.

After the meeting dismissed, Sean approached me. "Thanks for stepping up, Max. I'm really impressed."

I smiled. "Anything to help the team, boss."

Sean shook his head with a laugh. Yeah, he knew me.

We stayed after the meeting. Besides the bosses, it was me, Chase, Amica, and Jon. We talked about the goals of the team and a few details. Chase didn't look at me. Not even once. He seemed pleasant enough, smiling at all the right times, but I'd gotten pretty good at noticing his tells. The clenching of his jaw. Those fingers tapping against his leg. Maybe I was reading it all wrong. I didn't really know him well enough to know for sure. But the idea of all that energy built-up waiting to come out in the tapping of those elegant fingers had me thinking thoughts that were not really appropriate when talking to supervisors.

"Max? Does that work for you?"

Caught again. Everyone except Chase turned to me. "Works for me." I smiled at them all as if I didn't have a care in the world. And really, I didn't. This couldn't have gone better if I'd planned it.

"Great. We'll see everyone back here at three tomorrow."

Despite Chase's attitude or maybe because of it, I was really looking forward to this. It was a way to get to know him better. A way to figure out what was beyond all that blond hair Chase sometimes liked to hide behind. And that turned into thinking about his hair and threading my fingers through it. Pulling it just enough to tip Chase's head back so I could devour his mouth.

Fuck. I had to stop thoughts like those. Because as much as I wished Chase would be up for a fling, I knew otherwise.

As I waited for everyone to file out, I noticed Chase hanging back. Did he want to talk to his supervisor? Maybe he was going to back out. Why did the thought disappoint me so much?

I forced myself to walk out and head to the lounge to get a soda. I needed some time and caffeine before going back to work. I realized too late that Chase stayed behind, not so he could talk to his sup but so he could follow me. I tested that theory by taking a convoluted route. Maybe Chase had a reason to head to the lounge. He followed me, not missing a beat. I glanced back at him as I turned the corner to go into the breakroom. A shudder went through me at the fierce look on his face. Shit. This wasn't going to be good.

Thankfully, the room was empty because as soon as I reached the small room they sold sodas and snacks in, Chase grabbed my arm. So much for boundaries.

"What the fuck is your problem?"

I stared at him in shock. Of all the times Chase had snapped at me, he had never lost his cool. Not like this. His eyes flashed as he leaned closer jabbing me in the chest and breaking that protective bubble twice in less than a minute.

"My life is not a game for you to play. I am not here for your amusement."

I tried to step back, away from all that intensity aimed at me, but I had nowhere to go. The little dorm fridge holding the sodas dug into my back. I was unprepared for the passion radiating off him. Damn, angry looked good on him. The man was stunning.

"I want an explanation," he continued. "What the fuck is wrong with you? The question is not rhetorical."

"Okay, um, hold on..." I held up a hand, not sure what to say. *I'm a little bit obsessed with you.* Probably not the best way to start.

Chase shook out his hands possibly to dispel the electrical current hidden underneath that cool façade. "Answer me, Maxwell." My name on his lips sounded like sin.

I brought up both hands, trying to calm him down. "Maybe if you stepped back, I could think," I said. "This is my bubble..." I pointed around me.

"Don't you dare." His voice was low and dangerous.

"Look, Chase. I'm sorry I dragged you into it. I honestly thought you'd be interested. Turnover has been crazy around here."

"I'm not buying it," he said, crossing his arms and tilting

his head. "You've been fixated on me for some reason. Trying to take me down or something? Make me look like an idiot?"

"No that is not what I'm doing." I tried to show him I was sincere, but was I really? Wasn't that exactly what I was trying to do? Or had my intentions changed? I wanted to get to know him. That would help me figure out how to beat him. Right? "Maybe I just want to be friends." But who was I trying to convince?

"I don't believe you."

"Can't we call a truce?"

"That would imply there's a war going on." He indicated between the two of us. "This thing you have going on, it's been all one-sided."

"You attacked me."

"I've tried ignoring you, but if it's a fight you want, then let's go, because I don't let anyone, not even cute preppy boys who think they're all that, push me around."

"You think I'm cute?"

Chase gave me one last withering look. "I'm done being nice."

"Wait, this was you being nice?" But I was talking to his back. I could tell by the straight spine, he'd heard me. I watched him leave, enjoying the extra sway in his ass. I should have been worried. This was not the way to get on his good side. But the challenge in Chase's eyes was so fucking tempting, I couldn't resist.

My last call before lunch had run late, so Dylan had finished by the time I made it to the lunchroom. I wasn't sure I could hold up my side of a conversation anyway. My thoughts were focused on Chase. I had just finished my PB&J and was eating grapes when Amica sat down beside me. I'd been so preoccupied; I didn't even notice her approach. She'd heated up lasagna and the smell had me rethinking the ease of having a sandwich every day. She'd volunteered for the mentoring project. Maybe she wanted to discuss it. She was Chase's friend and had never sat with me before. Amica was gorgeous with cocoa-colored skin and a sweet smile. Of course, I was mostly unaffected by her charms. She was well-liked in the office. I nodded for her to take a seat.

"I was pretty impressed today, Max," Amica said. "Your ideas for mentoring were brilliant. Frankly it was hard to believe you came up with it." Her half smile told me she was mostly joking. "But did you see Chase's face when you volunteered him? Wow." She shook her head as she took a bite of her food. "Not sure I'd want to be in your shoes."

"He's not too happy with me."

"He doesn't like attention, and you singled him out." She pointed her fork at me. "Probably not the best idea."

"I just don't get it," I said, glad to finally have someone to talk to about this. "He's the number one customer service rep. He seems proud of that, and he gets a lot of attention for it."

"He's proud of his work. That doesn't mean he wants everyone's attention on him all at once. Chase is a very private guy. There's a fine line there."

"And I crossed it."

"You trampled it."

I hung my head. I'd focused so much on what I wanted, that I'd put Chase in a bad spot. I also didn't want Amica to hate me. "That wasn't my intention," I said. "I thought he'd be good at it and that it would be fun to work with him.

She smiled. "Got a little crush there?"

"No, not at all." I shook my head, knowing by her grin I was not convincing. It wasn't really a crush, even though I was attracted to him, and I looked forward to spending more time with him. "Do you think you can help me..."

"Get on Chase's good side?"

"Gain his trust so he'll at least talk to me. Obviously, that's something I need to do myself but maybe help smooth the way a little. You guys are friends, right?"

"Sort of. We don't really spend that much time together."

"But he likes you better than anyone else here."

"True," she said, tapping her finger on her chin in thought.

"If I get to the point that he tolerates me, I'll be happy." Would he really, though? Did he want more than that?

"You're asking for a lot, Max. Let me think about it."

"Sure," I said. "Thanks." I smiled, piling on the charm. We gossiped about various coworkers for the rest of the time. I'd never hung out with her before, but Amica was a lot of fun. We had tidied up and were about to leave when Chase walked in.

"This is not good," I said.

Amica turned, noticing Chase and waving him over.

"What are you doing?"

"Relax. This is perfect."

"What if he thinks we're conspiring against him?" I tried not to panic as Chase walked toward us, glaring at me.

"The best way to not look guilty is to not be guilty, Max. We've done nothing wrong."

"Tell that to him," I grumbled.

She had a big smile on her face as Chase reached us.

"Hi, Amica," he said with a smile. He turned to me and his smile vanished. "Maxwell."

"We were just discussing our new project," she said. "Care to join us?"

Chase hesitated before sitting down with his lunch.

My pulse jumped up, unbidden at the thought of being this close to Chase without him yelling at me. It surprised me that Chase would be okay with this. I silently thanked Amica.

"Why don't we get together tonight and talk about it?" she continued, not needing input from either of us. "We can invite Jon. It'll be a lot easier than trying to fit it in with work. We can even do it at my place?"

A flash of panic crossed Chase's face. I only noticed it because I was watching him so closely. "I don't know," he said.

"It's just a few of us," Amica said. "You've been to my place before, but if there's someplace else you want to meet, we can do that."

Chase took a deep breath, stretching his fingers out. "Your place is fine," he said amicably. "Is there anything you want me to bring?"

"If there's anything specific you'd like to snack on, otherwise just your cute little self."

Chase smiled shyly, his dimples showing. Who knew he had dimples? Not I. Probably because he never smiled in my direction. But now they could never be unseen.

"What about you, Max?"

"I'll be there. Just email me your address. I'll bring my famous queso dip."

"What makes it famous?" Chase asked. It was the first time he'd talked to me without malice in his voice. It threw me off guard for a second. He raised an eyebrow at me.

"I guess you'll just have to try it to find out." Was I really flirting with Chase? Wow. What a difference a few hours and an Amica made. I checked my watch and realized my time was almost up. "I have to go," I said, standing up. I hated to leave with Chase being friendly or at least not glaring at me like I was his sworn enemy.

"See you tonight." Amica winked at me. Chase didn't say anything, but he wasn't glaring. I took it as a win.

"What are you smiling at?" Dylan whispered as I settled into my desk.

"Nothing, except I have a non-date with Chase tonight." I grinned like an idiot, but I couldn't help it.

"What the heck is a non-date?"

"We're meeting at Amica's to plan for the mentorship thing."

Dylan shook his head. "You're going to be at the same place as him, and he's going to tolerate your presence. Is that what you're telling me?"

"I said it was a non-date, and right now tolerating is what I'm going for."

Dylan laughed, rolling his eyes. "You're pathetic."

I ignored him as my phone started buzzing. I didn't care what he thought. I was finally going to see Chase after work in a different environment. This was my chance to get to know him better. If I didn't screw it up.

SIX
Chase

I SWIPED THE SWEAT OFF MY FOREHEAD with the back of my hand, pushing away the strands of hair that had escaped my braid. The baseboards in the kitchen gleamed, but I still had the bathroom to clean, and the person ringing the doorbell was not going away. I sighed, pulling off my rubber gloves. There was no sense in ignoring it. It was most likely my sister. She'd called earlier to ensure I would be at the girls' dance recital on Saturday, and although I had tried to keep my voice even, she always seemed to know when I was stressed out. She'd been good at picking up on it when we were kids, and she seemed even better at it now. She said it was the twin thing; I just thought she liked to insert herself into my life. I threw the gloves in the sink and dusted the powder from my hands. I needed to wash them, but the doorbell was driving me crazy. And now she was knocking.

"Chase, I know you're in there," she said through the door.

I walked over to the back door and opened it. She brushed by me, talking the whole way.

"What's up?"

"Nothing. I'm just cleaning the baseboards."

"The baseboards? It must be worse than I thought."

"I don't know what you mean," I said, closing the door. I washed my hands in the sink while she continued talking.

"Chase, anytime you get stressed, you clean." She put her hands on her hips, staring me down. To be fair, that always worked when we were kids.

"No I don't. I just like things to be clean."

"Tell me all about it."

"I'm fine." Even as I denied it, I knew there was no point. She would get it out of me. She always did. And I could use someone to talk to.

Once we were seated in the living room with beverages, she started again. "What's going on?"

"It's nothing."

"We've already established that that's not true. So, could we move past the part where you deny, and I try to get you to talk? Just tell me."

"You're very pushy," I said. "You always have been. Even when we were kids."

"I'm your older sister. That's my job."

"You're older by five minutes." But she'd been the leader ever since. "Don't you have kids of your own to bother?"

"Is it a guy?"

Damn. Now I was thinking about Max and blushing. "It's not a guy," I said, unconvincingly.

"It's always a guy."

"No. In fact, it's never a guy. I haven't dated in two years. Not seriously."

"But that look on your face is the same one you'd get when Cameron riled you up. You cleaned your house and then came over and cleaned my house."

"The only reason I cleaned your house was because that's the place he was not at. He drove me crazy."

"Who's driving you crazy these days?"

I sighed. She would never give up. Resistance was futile. "If you must know, his name is Maxwell."

"And you like him?"

"No." I shook my head. "He's my coworker."

"But you want him to be more?"

"No. Are you going to let me tell it, or are you just going to make up your own version?"

She seemed to think about it for a moment. "Fine, go ahead," she said, taking a sip of her diet soda. "But at least make it interesting."

"This guy, Maxwell, always seems to be competing with me at work. We were in a team meeting today, and he volunteered for something and then volunteered me to help him."

"I like this guy."

"No. No we do not like this guy."

"Are you sure?"

This was why I didn't want to talk to my sister. She jumped to conclusions, not caring if there was truth to it. But she listened to me and had been very supportive during the whole Cameron thing.

"He's loud and outgoing and..."

"Charming?" She watched me closely. I could never hide from her.

"Sure. He's charming, but in an obnoxious way. Everybody loves him."

"Except for you."

"It's not that I dislike him. He pulls these pranks. He especially likes to pull them on me."

"Aww," she said. "It's like the little boy on the playground trying to get the little girl's attention by pulling on her pigtails."

"I am not a little girl with pigtails."

"You're not a little girl—"

"I do not have pigtails."

She glanced at my hair, and I self-consciously tossed the braid over my shoulder. "This is to keep my hair out of my face. It's not the same."

"I still think he likes you."

"Stop reading all those romance books, Sunny. They're warping your brain." I took a drink of my tea, trying to calm my pulse. Just thinking about Maxwell stressed me out.

"Trying to convince me? Or yourself?"

"Seriously, I don't think he's interested in me in that way. In fact, I don't even think he's gay. The first time we met, he hit on me."

"Sounds gay to me."

"He saw me from behind and thought I was a woman."

"Are you sure?"

"Yes." I didn't want to tell her how I knew. That the look on his face was disappointment and the realization of a huge mistake. I hoped she wouldn't press the issue.

"Okay, so he's not interested in your pigtails. What does he want?"

"I don't honestly know. The man's exhausting." And exciting. But I couldn't admit that or the fact that there were times when I enjoyed sparring with him. "And very intelligent." I felt more alive around him. As if I was important enough to be a challenge to him. I could barely explain it to myself.

"You could use someone like that in your life," she said, her tone serious.

"I despise the man."

"That doesn't sound like a no."

"He can be interesting, I guess," I said. "But now we're in this group together, and I have no idea how it's going to work out."

Her face lit up, and I held up my hand. "Do not start

matchmaking, Sunny. We are not together. We will never be together."

"So, he's not cute?"

"I didn't say that."

"Tell me more about him."

"No. I'm not doing that." I would not, under any circumstances, gush about Maxwell Sloan. No way. Sure, the guy was handsome, gorgeous even. But he was also arrogant and overbearing.

"What's the problem? You know he's not Cameron."

"Close enough," I said. Guys like Maxwell and Cameron were all the same. They were full of themselves and loud, very loud. Even if Maxwell wasn't like that, even if he wasn't Cameron, he still drew a lot of attention, not just because of his boisterous attitude; he was charming and extremely good-looking. Everyone's attention naturally went to him and that was not something I wanted to be around. I didn't want all that attention on me, and I would never put myself in that position again.

She put down her drink and took my hand. I shook my head, fighting back tears and any questions she had.

"I forgot the cookies. Do you want lemon or chocolate chip?" Thankfully, she let me leave the room without saying anything about the fact that I also baked. Cleaning and baking were my go-to stress relievers. I returned with the sweets and put them in front of her. She nibbled on a lemon cookie while I thought of what to say.

"We're all meeting tonight to plan."

"How many are in the group?"

"Four."

"Cozy."

"Sunny," I said. "Don't start."

She smiled at me. "Is there anything I can do to help?"

"Yes, you can take that scheming look off your face and

help me figure out what I'm going to wear. Should I just wear what I wore to work or should I go more casual?"

"It's not a date, right?"

"Definitely not a date."

"Then why are you so nervous, baby brother?"

"Shut up."

"I definitely think you should wear the braid."

I combed my fingers through my hair as I walked up the steps to Amica's apartment. I'd been here before when she needed help with a project she'd been working on. Although I was nervous just being away from home and around others, I had to admit, the main reason for my anxiety was Maxwell. I longed to be back in my kitchen, broom in hand. When I was cleaning, it was easy to put order in my life. If something was dirty, just clean it up. If only life could be that way. Something messy in your life? Grab a broom. A mop. But it wasn't that easy. People weren't that easy.

I took a deep breath. I could do this. I'd done it before. It would be good for me to get out. Now I sounded like my sister. Maybe Max and I could work something out so there wasn't all this tension between us. Tension that had been there since the first moment we met.

I rang the doorbell, my heart racing and my stomach twisting in knots. Sunny had helped me with my outfit. I looked the perfect amount of casual and business. I didn't want anyone to forget this meeting was work-related. But I also didn't want to come off as stuck up.

As I'd cleaned, I thought about the mentoring thing. It really was a good idea, and it could help the company. It would look good on my resume, if I decided to get another job or move up in the company. I wouldn't tell Maxwell that. He'd make my life unbearable. And I could make him suffer as long as possible. I didn't mind the actual work. It was the loss of control in that moment when he'd volunteered me. I couldn't say no in front of all those people. And I hated controlling men. I shook off the cobwebs from the past, as Amica opened the door with a cheerful smile.

The meeting started off well. Maxwell charmed everyone but was more subdued than I'd ever seen him. There were only four of us, so there were several times when it was just Maxwell and me. He'd insisted I call him Max. He said Maxwell was his father's name.

A half-hour into the meeting, Max and I were arguing over the best way to provide the mentorship. Max thought it would be best for the mentors to be on the call with the new workers, assisting them as needed and taking notes to share later.

"Isn't that what the supervisor does?" I asked.

"But it would be on an informal basis. Not as scary." Max had Venn diagramed his ideas, and I thought it was a little cute. He was really trying.

"Some people don't do well in that situation," I said. "They have performance anxiety."

Max laughed. "So, you know all about performance anxiety, Chase?"

My face heated as I realized what I'd said. Amica and Jon sat in chairs at the small table off of the kitchen. It wasn't a big apartment, and I could see them looking over at us. Jon with interest and Amica with concern. I shook my head and smiled. I wasn't offended by the comments Max had made. Just a little embarrassed.

My face was probably beet red with my fair coloring. Max smiled, his eyes crinkling up with laughter.

"You know what I mean, Max," I said, willing the blush to leave my face.

"I do. I was just joking with you."

And the funny thing was I did feel like it was a joke shared between us, and not a joke at my expense. We'd been having a good conversation so far. I didn't want to ruin it. "I'm just saying it might be better to do role-playing."

"You like role playing?"

"Please stop making everything sexual."

Which only made Max laugh even harder.

"I'm going to get me another drink." I started to stand up when Max touched my arm.

"Hey, I'm sorry. Sometimes I act like a juvenile."

"Delinquent?"

"That's fair," Max conceded.

"I'm just getting a drink. Anyone else want anything?"

They all shook their heads, and I headed to the kitchen to get another glass of iced tea. I was thirsty, but I mostly needed a moment to myself. Max didn't get the hint. I could tell he was behind me as I reached into the fridge, but I didn't acknowledge his presence.

"Seriously, I didn't mean to embarrass you."

I poured tea into my glass, trying to keep my hand steady. "Really, it's fine," I said. And I meant it. I wasn't mad at Max. At all. In fact, part of the problem was that Max was making sexual innuendos and had me flustered more than embarrassed.

"I want to apologize."

"Max, I told you it's fine."

"No, not about sex jokes..."

Really did he have to keep talking about sex? It had been a long time for me. And I didn't need the reminder. It was enough that Max was standing over me, oozing sex appeal. I cleared my throat, trying to get my head straight.

"I was an ass to you, Chase," he said. "I shouldn't have volunteered you for this. I realize how hard that was for you."

And although I was trying to listen to his apology and be a

grown up about this, Max being so close to me and using words like ass and hard... What the hell was wrong with me? I turned back to the counter and tried to will my inappropriate reaction away.

"Chase..." And then he touched me. His hand broke through my protective bubble and rested on my arm for just a second. My skin tingled from the contact, and I wanted those strong hands touching me everywhere.

I needed to get control of myself and the situation. Max was such a paradox. He could be arrogant and annoying but also sweet and caring. I studied the dirty dishes in the sink. Would it be weird if I started washing them? Probably.

"Do you want some more tea?" Which was a strange question since Max had been drinking Diet Coke. That he'd brought. But if he noticed how crazy I was acting, he didn't say anything about it.

"No, thanks."

Once we were settled back in the living room, we worked out a plan that included both our ideas. I was so into it I couldn't help the excitement in my voice.

"This will be great," I said. "We can tailor it to each individual's needs."

Max shook his head.

"What?"

"I've never seen you this animated," he said. "It looks good on you."

I tried not to blush, but it was no use. Was Max flirting with me? Doubtful. But I still enjoyed his attention on me. It was like I was the only person in the room. I usually didn't like attention, but I could get addicted to this feeling and that was dangerous.

Max's phone rang, and I started taking notes on my paper so it didn't seem like I was listening. He sighed at the person on the other end, closing his eyes in frustration.

"Fine," he said. "Put him on." He walked away as if he was afraid I'd hear the other person. "Toby." His voice was strong and commanding. "They're just people. Stop being so anxious all the time. Just get over it. We've talked about this." He walked into the kitchen to finish his conversation.

My heart pounded so hard I could feel the blood whooshing through my brain. Was this the real Max Sloan? How could he talk to someone like that? Especially someone with anxiety? It made me feel sick to my stomach. Is this what he thought of me? I almost left, but I wouldn't give him the satisfaction. Max might have everyone else fooled, but not me. I've seen guys like this before, and I would never put up with it again.

SEVEN

Max

THINGS HAD BEEN GOING GREAT AT OUR impromptu meeting. Everyone loved my queso dip, and Chase and I worked out a plan we were both proud of. I didn't want to leave, but Toby was freaking out. Couldn't he have kept his issues under control for just one evening? Was that really too much to ask?

Chase had really been warming up to me, but by the time I started saying my goodbyes, he was again giving me the cold shoulder. I had no idea what that was about. I mean, I'd been joking around with him about sex, but I thought he was enjoying our banter. I went over every detail of the evening, trying to figure out where it all went wrong. But I couldn't figure it out. Unless it was just that I was leaving early. I obsessed over it during the ride home but finally I had to give up. It wasn't helpful at all.

I could hear Toby before I even opened the door. Once I was inside, he rushed my feet, barking hysterically.

"Toby," I said. "You know it's me. There's absolutely no reason to bark." I threw my satchel on the dining room table, then scooped the dog into my hands. "My little Tobi-wankenobi. Come on, buddy, it's not that bad." I scratched his ears. He had light tan and white curls around his face and sweet brown eyes. I loved snuggling with him. I carried him to the couch to chill out and spoke soft words to him. It wasn't his fault. Toby had always had a problem with barking. He was the protector in the family and was ready to attack anyone who came to the door. Or anyone who knocked on the door. Or anyone who happened to walk by the door. He sometimes even barked at the people on the street. And we lived on the third floor.

He was a terrier mix. A small ball of spitfire. He'd gotten better about the barking and being nervous, but anything that threw him off his routine, like me going out in the evening once I'd been home, spiked his anxiety. The vet had even given me some anti-anxiety pills for when he was really messed up. It was a problem, not only because Toby's barking could get us thrown out of the apartment building, but because he licked at things all the time, causing sores on his little body.

I kissed the top of his head. "Don't worry, Tobers. We're in for the night." I changed into sweatpants, Toby following at my heels. I loved my little dog even if he was a pain in the ass. When the neighbor had called, all I could think about was not wanting to end my time with Chase. And that was selfish. It wasn't Toby's fault that there was a change in his routine. He'd probably heard steps in the hallway, causing him to bark for thirty minutes straight. My neighbor Janice was a sweet lady and always willing to help me out. The last thing we needed was to get thrown out of our apartment because of Toby's excessive barking. She held the phone up to the door, hoping that Toby hearing my voice would calm him down. It had worked some. But I couldn't stay any longer, even though I hated the thought of leaving Chase when we'd just developed an almost friendship. But my dog came first.

As I settled in my chair with a beer and Toby on my lap,

watching the newest show on Netflix, I couldn't help my mind going back to Chase. It was like I was finally getting to see the real guy. This side of him reminded me of the guy I talked to on the phone when I pretended to be a customer. Chase was still that sarcastic, fiery, irritating guy from work, but the fact that he wasn't perfect made it perfect. I shut my eyes, shaking my head. What was it about this one guy that had me so captivated? He was a challenge, yes, and that was enticing. It was probably just my attraction to him. Maybe I should call Leroy for another round... Wait, that wasn't his name. Lee?

But I wasn't interested in hooking up with anyone else. That more than anything made me realize that if I wasn't careful, I could actually fall for this guy.

The next day at work, it was as if we'd never met. Chase was back to ignoring me, and I had no idea what I'd done. After first break, I stopped Amica in the hallway.

"Hey, Am," I said. "Thanks for hosting last night. I thought things went well. I mean we got a plan together and that's good, right?" I couldn't look her in the eye. I didn't want it to be obvious that I was grilling her for information.

"What the hell did you do to Chase?" She crossed her arms and gave me a pointed stare.

"What you mean? Nothing." I tripped over my words, and she raised her eyebrows at me.

"Want to try that again?"

"I don't know," I said with a sigh. "Everything was going great and then I had to leave, and he seemed upset again. Did he say anything after I left?"

"No. He left almost immediately afterwards. But he was not happy. I thought maybe you said something to him."

"No. I mean yeah I talked to him. But he didn't seem upset until the end."

Amica stared in the direction of Chase's cubical. "Fine. I'll try to figure out what's going on. Meanwhile for the sake of our project, stay away from him."

"You don't think I should say I'm sorry?"

"You know what you're apologizing for?"

"Not a clue. But I'm sure it's me. It's usually me."

"Agreed."

"Hey," I said, a little offended.

"We both know it's true. But you can't apologize if you don't know what you're apologizing for. That will only piss him off even more."

As much as I hated to admit it, she was right. If I apologized to Chase, he would ask me what I was apologizing for, and I wouldn't have an answer. I had to let Amica do this. "See what you can find out. Then report back to me."

"I am not your damn spy. I'm going to see what's wrong with my friend. If there's something you can do to help, I'll let you know." And with that, she turned and left me standing there.

I noticed Chase going toward the lounge out of the corner of my eye. The urge to stop him, to make this right, was strong, but I promised Amica I would stay out of it for now. Chase raised his chin a bit. His body seemed to tighten up as he came closer. His fingers tapped furiously on his leg. Yep, he was still angry. Instead of engaging with him, I turned around and went back to my desk. My break was almost up. Dylan gave me a questioning look, his eyebrows raised. I shook my head. No way could I explain this to my friend. I felt like an idiot already.

EIGHT

Chase

WORK GROUNDED ME, GIVING ME SOMETHING to focus on besides Max. During the down times, when fewer calls were coming through, I'd think about how he'd talked to his friend, and it infuriated me. In contrast to his words, his tone had been warm but firm. He was obviously talking to someone he cared about. That only made it worse. It didn't bother me that he had someone in his life who trusted him so much he went to Max for help. Not much anyway. It reminded me of Cameron and the similar things he'd said to me almost daily. But interspersed among those awful thoughts were the other things Max had said. The way he had teased me, his voice warm and deep. My skin tingled at the memory of his touch on my arm. I blushed, thinking of what Max had said to me, the way he had leaned toward me, his gray-blue eyes watching me carefully. As if I was important to him. But then those hateful words would return. "It's just people. Why do you have to be so nervous all the time? Just get over it." It felt like a splash of cold water was being thrown on me. I shivered. Maybe I was getting sick. I didn't feel like I'd ever be warm again.

"They need to ban popcorn in here," Amica said, sitting down. The smell of burnt popcorn had escaped my notice when I'd entered the lunchroom. Another indication I was obsessed.

I nodded, not looking at her. I wasn't ready for company, but I didn't have the heart to push her away.

"Are you okay?" She tilted her head in concern. The last thing I wanted was her worrying about me. At least she kept her voice low.

"I'm fine." I smiled but the frown on her face told me it fell flat.

"I thought the meeting last night went well."

She probably thought changing the subject would cheer me up, but it did the opposite. It reminded me of Max. I tightened my fingers on my glass, trying to hold it together.

If Amica noticed, she ignored it. "Max had a lot of good ideas. That kind of surprised me."

Max was the last person I wanted to talk about, but the topic seemed inevitable. "I guess."

"You guys were hitting it off."

I sighed. "Maxwell Sloan can be charming," I admitted. "But he's also loud and arrogant, and I really don't want to talk about him."

"Did he say or do something..."

"I don't want to talk about it."

"You want me to hide all his paperclips?" She sounded serious, but her eyes were crinkled at the edges. Amica was a good friend. I wasn't sure I deserved her.

"He still uses paperclips?"

"He also has a stash of colorful gel pens."

"He does?" That surprised me, although it shouldn't. Max seemed like someone who liked colorful things in his life. Not gray depressing things. I shut those thoughts down.

"I can replace them with plain black ink pens. Or all one color."

I pretended to think about it, tilting my head to the side. "Maybe we should tape the wheels on his chair. He likes to roll around a lot."

"Chase," she said, her voice shocked. "That's brilliant. Who knew you could be so evil?"

I laughed, my tension melting away. I didn't need to stress over Maxwell. We'd put the proposal together. Maybe that would be the end of our association. I could probably get paired with Amica for the actual implementation.

Everywhere I went, Max was there. I wasn't sure if it was because I was now more aware of him, or if it was intentional. Maybe a little of both.

I ran into him in the hallway during my last break. Almost literally. I stopped just short of invading his bubble. The irony that it was because I was obsessing over him, wasn't lost on me.

"Chase," Max said. "Good to see you." His voice was calm and low. Unusually so.

I narrowed my eyes, remembering seeing him with Amica earlier in the day. "What did Amica tell you?"

"Nothing." He held his hands up defensively. "I just said hi to her."

"You're a terrible liar."

"Fine. She told me to stay away from you."

"Smart girl." My heart warmed at the thought of Amica being protective of me. It hit me then that I did have friends; I wasn't a complete failure at socializing.

"I'd like to point out that you are the one invading my space."

I had stepped closer to him without noticing it. Probably so no one could hear us. At least that was the reason I was going with. It had nothing to do with his magnetic personality. I backed up quickly, annoyed that he would point it out.

"Maybe we should get together and go over our proposal before presenting it to management. We can invite Amica and Jon."

"Just send it out by email. I don't have any time to meet." It wasn't a complete lie.

"What about during lunch tomorrow?"

"No," I said before turning and walking away. I had to be firm with him. I was done letting people talk me into things I didn't want to do.

The afternoon dragged on. I tried not to think of Max. All I wanted to do was go home and relax in my nice peaceful apartment. *Don't you mean boring*? I pushed that thought away. "I mean quiet."

"Are you talking to me?"

I glanced up at Gina. She had the cubby next to me and was on her way back to her desk. "No," I said. "I was talking to myself."

"Oh, okay," she said, giving me a strange look before slipping into her cubbyhole. Great. Now people would think I was crazy as well as stuck up. I blamed Max.

When I finally got home from work, I made a dish of fish and rice. It wasn't much fun cooking for one, especially since I loved to cook. Normally, I didn't even think much about it, but now I felt increasingly lonelier. I cleaned up and settled on the couch. I had a book I'd been reading, but I couldn't get into it. That wasn't surprising, but the fact that I wasn't thinking about Max was. Instead, my mind decided to focus on the whole Cameron debacle.

I tried to convince myself that Max and Cameron were nothing alike, but I was having a hard time believing it. Cameron and I had dated for a couple of years, then ended up moving in together. I thought we were serious. And maybe

Cameron did take our relationship seriously, but he didn't take me seriously. When we were out together, he liked to be the life of the party. People loved him. They flocked to him, and he loved showing me off, like I was a prize he'd won. I wasn't comfortable with the attention. Still, I grinned and went along with it. I thought I was being strong, overcoming this weakness called social anxiety. And I wanted Cameron to be happy. But it never got any easier.

Cameron thought I needed to try harder. It was my problem, not his. He put it all on my shoulders but occasionally, I would snap and say something to him. He always acted like it was a surprise that I still hadn't gotten over my issues. He thought I needed to take another pill. The medication helped; otherwise, I would not have been able to attend all the parties Cameron was invited to. He was a lawyer, and schmoozing was part of the job. I'd often become overwhelmed at social events and ask Cameron to take me home. He'd bitch about it but usually relented. I even suggested we take two cars in case I had a meltdown. Cameron acted like that was a stupid idea. He always made a scene about how I just needed another glass of wine and I'd be fine. It was like he didn't understand me at all or didn't want to understand me. But I stuffed it all down. I was defective and it was up to me to deal with it. I tried my best and often I worked harder at the relationship than Cameron. Maybe that wasn't fair.

I came to a breaking point one Friday evening when Cameron had gotten us tickets to a movie we both wanted to see. I had been so excited that he was doing something that didn't involve tons of other people. Something just for the two of us. That excitement evaporated once we reached the movie theater.

"Cam? Did you pick out our seats?"

"Yes," he said, pulling me through the crowded theater. "But they were packed so I didn't have a lot of choices."

We reached our row, which was full except for two seats in the middle. I focused on my breathing. I didn't want to make a scene. "You know I prefer the aisle or a seat against the wall."

"I know, babe. But these were the only good seats left."

Anger tightened through my body, but it wasn't anger at Cameron. It was at myself. Why couldn't I just sit next to a stranger in a movie theater like anybody else? Why did I have to be so fucking anxious about everything?

"I mean there were aisle seats up front," he said, "but you know that hurts my neck if I have to sit that close."

"I can't do this." I couldn't catch my breath. I closed my eyes, trying to ground myself.

"It's just a couple of hours," he said, a hint of anger in his voice. "Just try, okay?"

But I wasn't talking about the movie. I was talking about our relationship. Maybe I just wasn't strong enough. I just knew I'd had enough. I shook my head, stretching my fingers out to ease the tension.

"I'm so tired of having to do things your way, Chase." His voice rose and I cringed at the attention we were getting. "Life is messy. You need to learn how to deal with it."

In that moment, I hated everything. Myself for being so messed up. The people around me for staring at us. The fact that I couldn't sit in a movie theater in the dark for two hours next to a total stranger. But most of all, I hated Cameron for putting me in this position in the first place, knowing it would be difficult for me.

"Are we going to sit down or what?" Cameron asked when I hadn't said anything. "Or we can go if you want."

"Go ahead and sit down," I said. His passive aggressiveness wasn't working this time. I would not feel guilty about ruining our evening. "I'm going to get some air."

"Take some meds while you're at it."

I'd walked outside, and then proceeded to walk out of his

life. I'd gone home, packed up all my stuff and called Sunny. The girls were under five, and her husband, Brad, was working late, but she still packed them up and drove out to get me. She didn't talk most the way to her house. Once she got the kids to bed and we were alone, I broke down.

"Why am I such a freak?" I said. "Why can't I just be normal like everybody else?"

"It's not you, hun." She tipped my head up so I had to look at her. "Cam is an asshole."

We both laughed a little. I nodded, wiping the tears from my face. "You could have told me that sooner."

"You already knew."

I nodded again, crying on her shoulder.

Tears streamed down my face at the memory. I went to the bathroom and washed my face. I hated reliving those moments. I'd gone to therapy to work through the crap Cameron had put me through. And although I still had anxiety, I had learned that everyone struggled with something.

I made a vow to myself: Any man I became involved with would have to be someone who could accept me the way I was. Max's words on the phone that day came back to me. As charming as he was, I wasn't going to fall for Max Sloan. I could resist him. I had to. There was no way I would ever do that to myself again.

NINE

Max

I USUALLY LOVED THE WEEKENDS. Hanging out with friends and family, and maybe even a little extra time in the gym. I was always busy. But not this weekend. Dylan and Sadie had gone out of town to visit her family. I didn't feel like doing anything. I spent most of the weekend sitting at home with Toby, binging Netflix.

As long as I watched something, I could keep my mind off Chase. That was the theory, anyway. It didn't quite work out because the man was always on my mind. I couldn't figure out what I'd done to set him off. We'd been getting along so well. At least I thought so. When I tried to talk to him on Friday, he was cold and dismissive. I was back where I started. I might've even lost ground. There was nothing I could do, so I needed to stop obsessing about it.

Sunday afternoon Toby and I went over to my parents' house. During the summer months, they liked to have barbecues. All the time. My whole family was usually there. I had three brothers, an older sister, and a younger sister, and they would usually all bring their families. It was a lot of people. There were a few that lived out of state or traveled. But mostly they were all expected to show up. I didn't really feel like being around people, but my sister Carole would hunt me down. On orders from my mom. Two women I really didn't want to disappoint.

I helped Howard man the grill. Actually, I was avoiding my sister. She could read me like a book. Toby ran off to explore the area.

"Are you hiding?"

"No," I said, trying not to sound guilty.

"Then do something useful and hand me that plate."

We talked about football starting soon and who had the best team. Howard could tell something was bothering me, but his way of dealing with it was different from his wife. He'd just try to distract me. That was why he was one of my favorites.

"Is Josh here?" My younger brother studied at Florida State University, but since it was the summer, I thought he'd be home.

"He didn't get the internship he wanted."

Josh wanted to be a marine biologist. His main problem seemed to be that he was afraid of water. "Why doesn't he choose another profession?"

"Sloan stubbornness?"

I couldn't argue with that. We were a stubborn bunch. Carole was the oldest, and I was a year younger than her. Then came Josh. Jamie and Henry were in their early twenties and Greta was the baby. She just graduated from high school. "Is he hiding?"

"He's supposed to be here. But you know your sister. Carole will drag his ass back here if he doesn't show up."

I hated that Josh was having problems, but maybe it would keep everyone off my ass.

Everyone devoured the food. Toby hung around the younger kids, hoping for scraps. Howard added a secret ingredient to his barbecue sauce. No one knew what it was except for Carole. Mom and Dad smiled on, proud of their big family. Josh even snuck in. I didn't draw any attention to it, but I handed him a beer. "Looks like you could use this."

He smiled. "Thanks."

Avoiding the subject of school, I asked him about his boyfriend, Liam.

Josh sighed. "He's in Australia right now. I'm supposed to go over there for Christmas break." He shrugged. "We talk all the time, but long distance is hard. How's your love life? Dating anyone? Or just hooking up?"

I thought of Chase but shook my head. I didn't count Levi or whatever his name was. That was one night and not even worth repeating. "No one in particular."

Thankfully, he didn't call me on it.

"Are we playing football?" Jamie asked, running up to us. He was the star quarterback of the family. He'd played all through high school and now played at MU.

"Sure," I said. "I'm in." At least physical activity would help keep my mind off Chase.

After getting tackled multiple times and hit with the ball, I realized my mistake. You should only play football with the Sloan family if your head was in the game. Mine wasn't.

"What is up with you?"

I tried to ignore my sister. It was futile. Carole didn't give up easily. "Mac? Answer me."

When I was little, Carole had trouble with my name. It came out as Mac instead of Max and it stuck ever since. Which worked out fine since my dad's name was also Maxwell.

"Nothing," I said. "It's nothing."

"Is it work?"

"No. Work is fine."

"Oh, my gosh! It's a guy isn't it? Please tell me it's guy."

"Why?" I stared at her, nursing my bruised arm. Those

guys could really tackle. The game played on without me. "Why would you want it to be a guy?"

"Tell me first if it is."

"Fine," I said with a sigh. "It's a guy. Now tell me why."

"Because I've never seen you this preoccupied over anything unless it's work. You telling me it's a guy tells me all I need to know."

I shook my head, trying to ignore the big smile on her face. "I changed my mind. I don't want to talk to you."

"No, you can't change your mind," she said. "I have to know who this guy is that has enchanted my sweet but always unavailable brother."

"What does that even mean?"

"It means you go through men like I go through underwear."

"Can we not talk about your underwear? Gross."

"Fine then, socks. You go through men like I go through socks. Better?"

"Marginally." I glanced around to make sure no one else could hear us. "His name is Chase."

"Wait... Is this the guy that you are always trying to beat for customer service rep?"

"Forget it."

She grabbed my hand to keep me from moving. "No, don't go anywhere. Talk to me. I've been waiting for this moment since you stole my boyfriend junior year."

"I gave him back."

"Stop stalling and talk."

I needed to talk to someone, and it was getting increasingly harder to talk to Dylan about this. And although Carole might rib me about it for the rest of my life, I could trust her. She had always been there for me. She encouraged me at fifteen to come out to mom and dad. I'd been terrified, but she assured me it would be okay. And it was.

She'd been tall for her age. Taller than all the other boys. She always threatened anyone who even thought about making fun of me. And while as a kid I didn't really appreciate that support, as an adult I recognized how awesome it was to have her on my side.

"At first," I said, "I just wanted to figure out how he always got the top customer rep when he was so antisocial toward everyone in the office. I just couldn't figure it out. What was so great about this guy? And then we were thrown together on a project, and I got to know him better." I didn't mention using her husband, Howard's, account to call Chase. She would be disappointed in me.

"What changed?"

I kicked at the grass, thinking about how to answer that. "I saw a whole new side of him. He's an introvert, so the complete opposite of me, but that's what makes him interesting. When he lets me see the real him, it's like he's giving me something special."

"Are you in love with this guy?"

I looked up at her, startled by her question. "I barely know him. But there is something about him."

"Way to avoid the question. Does he know you're interested?"

I laughed at that. "I'm not even sure he knows I'm gay."

"How is that possible?"

"It's not like I broadcast it at work. And the first time I saw him... He has this long beautiful hair. Let's just say he thinks I thought he was a girl."

"Did you think he was a girl?"

I shrugged. "Maybe for a second. But then my eyes wandered past the hair to those muscular thighs and that ass. I knew he was a guy before he turned around. What shocked me was the pure look of contempt on his face. It was like he knew me and already hated me. I stepped back and pretended I made a mistake. It seemed easier that way."

"Are you going to tell him you're gay?"

"We're no longer on speaking terms. So, I'm not sure what the point would be. I don't even know what I did wrong to piss him off."

"Do you want my advice?"

"Does it matter?" I asked.

"No."

"Okay give me your brilliant assessment."

"My advice is don't give up," Carole said. "I haven't seen you this interested in anyone in a very long time. You deserve to be happy, Mac. All your life you've gone from one guy to the next, never wanting to settle down. I'm not sure what that's about, but for you to finally be interested in someone for more than just hooking up, that guy must be special. Don't give up on him."

"Thanks, sis," I said.

"No problem. You can return the favor by helping me set up the slip and slide to keep the kiddos entertained."

It was a relief to have confided in someone, but her words haunted me. What if Chase and I did get together? Would I panic and end up hurting him? I've never wanted to settle down, and Chase wasn't the type to just hook up. Would there be any future for us? I wasn't sure but the thing was...this was the first time I really wanted to try.

This might be one of the stupidest things I've ever done, and I've done plenty of stupid things. I rubbed my eyes, trying to get my brain to think logically. Maybe if I did that, if I thought hard enough, I could talk myself out of this crazy idea.

It had been a week since I last spoke to Chase. I had tried.

But every time I got close to him, Chase turned and walked the other way, pretending he didn't even see me.

We'd had another meeting to present our proposal to management. Chase hadn't even looked at me. And when they'd teamed us together to troubleshoot the challenges management had brought up, Chase made sure he was with Amica. That should've been the end of it. It was clear that Chase was not interested in me, even as a friend. It was obvious that I'd done something, said something, that alienated him.

I'd told myself I just needed to know what I'd done, but that wasn't the reason. I had a taste of what it was like to be friends with Chase, to have that connection to him, and I wanted more of that. And if I was completely honest with myself, I wanted more than friendship. I wanted to hold him, to run my fingers through all that glorious hair. To pull him into a kiss and wipe all his fears away.

Chase could be both acidic and sweet and one without the other wasn't working for me anymore. I wanted the whole package. But I wasn't getting either, right now. I was getting the silent treatment. I'd even be okay with Chase bitching me out some more. Which was why I was desperate enough to do something I should not be doing. Something that could actually cost me my job.

I wanted to talk to Chase again and the only way I could do that was by calling him again using my brother-in-law's name. The first time had been less risky because I hadn't talked to Chase much so there wasn't much of a chance he would recognize my voice. Even if he had thought it sounded like me, he wouldn't have believed it.

We'd talked for hours that night. Chase would probably recognize my voice this time. And if he did, he would assume I was harassing him. There was a chance he would go to his boss and complain about me. This would not end well for me and that was the absolute reason I couldn't do it. No matter how much I wanted to. Yet I couldn't stop my fingers from dialing the number.

The first time I called, it went to someone else. That only happened if the person was on a call or on a BRB. Chase had already taken his afternoon break. I felt like a stalker. This was a sign that I was doing something I shouldn't. I waited ten minutes and ignored the sign.

"Thank you for calling Coxx Communications. This is Chase. How can I help you?"

The sweetness of his voice, the intimacy of hearing it in my ear, as if Chase was whispering to me, caught me off guard. My mouth was so dry I had to take a drink of my water.

"Hello is there anyone there?"

"Yes," I said, taking a calming breath. "Sorry, yes this is Howard Hernandez. I called before. I'm having trouble with my Internet." I tried to keep my voice as low as possible so Chase wouldn't recognize it. I wasn't sure it was working but so far, he hadn't bitched me out. I'd take that as a win.

"Okay, I can help with that. What's your account number?"

I rattled off Howard's information and waited for Chase to bring up the notes from his last call. As long as Howard never actually had trouble with his Internet, I'd be fine.

"Oh," he said, clearing his throat. "I remember you. Have you checked that it's not on airplane mode?" There was amusement in his voice.

"First thing I did." I laughed nervously. Chase must think I'm an idiot. Which I obviously was.

"Are you having trouble connecting to your laptop or your phone?"

"I can't connect to either." My heart pounded so loud I was afraid he could hear it. I was such an idiot, but I had the answer to my question. It was definitely worth it. Chase's voice softened as he troubleshooted the Internet connection problem with me, like he was enjoying the conversation. That was probably all in my head, but I'd take what I could get.

"Okay, Mr. Hernandez..."

"Mac."

"Excuse me?"

"You can call me Mac."

"Mac," he said, his voice sounding a little shy. "Now turn your laptop back on."

The way he said my nickname sent inappropriate signals to my cock. Now was not the time to get an erection. My body disagreed. Chase whispering things in my ear, even though they were computer-related, or maybe because they were computer-related had me hard in an instant. I was definitely going to get myself fired. And why was I giving him so much information? But did it matter? Chase was never planning on talking to me again. Maybe this was all I'd ever get.

"Is it working?"

Yes. "No," I said.

"Are the lights on your router lit up?"

"Which one is the router again?" I could tell Chase was fighting back a comment, re-evaluating how much his customer knew. We got people like this all the time. They just didn't understand the difference between a router and modem or technology in general. Of course, I wasn't one of those people. I just needed Chase to think I was.

"Your modem is what you get from us," he said patiently. "And your router is what sends out your Wi-Fi signal."

"Oh, okay. So it's the tall thingy? I don't see any lights."

"Wait," Chase said, his voice wary. "I thought we checked that it was turned on."

"It was," I said. Shit. I didn't need him getting suspicious. Why was I dragging it out, anyway? He'd fixed my "problem." I just wanted a few more minutes with him.

"I'm sorry," I said, trying to sound apologetic. "I think I stepped on the surge protector and shut if off again. I turned it back on. The lights are flashing now."

"It may take a few minutes for your Wi-Fi to connect."

"Do you like your job, Chase?"

"What?"

"Well, you said we had a few minutes. Do you like your job?"

"I do. I like helping people. Technology can be frustrating to some. And I know what it's like to be frustrated."

"You're very good at your job." I couldn't believe he was sharing so much with me. Would he be this open if he knew it was me? Definitely not.

"Thank you, Mac. Is your Wi-Fi working now?"

"Let me check." I waited a few seconds. "Yep, Google comes up now. Thanks."

"Any time. Is there anything else I can help you with today?"

That was my cue to end the call, but I just didn't want to.

"I have a question about the different cable packages. I'm thinking of changing mine to the next level." I knew Chase wouldn't let it go on for too long. We were encouraged to get calls completed within fifteen minutes, especially if the problem was already fixed. "Can I get NFL Redzone with that?"

"Yes, absolutely," he said. "I can connect you to our cable representatives if you want more information. They would know more than I would."

"That's okay," I said. "Whatever you know is fine. I mean I can always look it up, right?"

"Yes. You can go to our website and check that out."

"Now that I have my Wi-Fi working?"

"Yes," Chase said with a laugh. "Now that your modem is plugged in and you're not on airplane mode, you should be fine. It just makes me wonder what issue you'll be having next week."

Fuck. I was caught. But I didn't think he knew it was me. "Is it that obvious?" I asked.

"I do have people who are clueless about technology, but not often do I have the same person calling back for totally different reasons that they could've easily troubleshooted for themselves."

"Sorry," I said. "I just like the sound of your voice."

"Thank you," Chase said, "But it's probably not a good idea to call back unless you are actually having a problem."

"Maybe we could meet?" Why had I said that? It wasn't like we could really meet. I just got carried away.

"I'm sorry. I'm sure you're a nice guy but that's totally against the rules, and I like my job as I said, and I'd like to keep it."

"Right. Sorry. That was stupid. Very unprofessional of me."

"It's fine. I'm the one who has to be professional here, not you."

Later after I'd gone to bed, I replayed every word he said. Was Chase flirting with me? Part of me enjoyed it and another part, the insane part, was jealous that he would flirt with a customer. I was a mess and it was all Chase Corrigan's fault.

TEN

Chase

I LATHERED MYSELF UP WITH SPF 50 SUNSCREEN. I burned easily, the curse of fair skin, and I wasn't taking that chance. Swimming wasn't on the list of my favorite things to do, but hanging out with Sunny and her family, was at the top, especially my nieces. I stretched out in the lounge chairs next to my sister while her husband, Brad, and the girls splashed around in the water.

"You look sullen today."

"I was going for aloof."

"You want to talk about it?"

"No." I put my sunglasses on and pretended to bask in the sun without a care in the world. She didn't buy it. I never could fool her.

When she didn't respond, I glanced over at her. She was watching me closely. Waiting for me to break.

"Okay, fine." I took my sunglasses off and sat up. I moved closer so we could talk without anyone else listening. Not that anyone there cared. They were enjoying the sun and water. Not pouting over a guy. "He's tried to talk to me a few times, but I just walked away." I'd already told her all about the little fiasco with the team meeting and Max's views on anxiety. She sympathized with me. She hated Cameron as much as I did. Possibly even more.

"Is he harassing you?"

"No. He stopped after that. I think he gave up."

"Maybe you should give him a chance, Chase."

"Why?"

"Friendship," she said. "Maybe more."

"I already have enough friends." Hopefully, she wouldn't challenge me on that one. Besides family, Amica was my only real friend. "As for more, I don't even know if he's gay."

"Really?" she said, her eyebrows raised. "You can't tell by the way he looks at you? Or the way he talks to you? It's not obvious?"

I sighed. "He's interested, I think. It feels like he is anyway, but he's never said he was gay..."

"Does he need to?"

"I can't go through that all over again, Sunny." I looked down, hiding behind my hair. I hated being so emotional all the time. I'd thought about this already. In fact, it was all I'd been thinking about for the last week. I was tired of thinking about Max, and definitely tired of thinking about Cameron and remembering the old pain. I figured my brain was just reminding me what a big mistake it would be to go down that road again.

But then the phone call from the customer on Friday popped in my mind. Talk to him. Laughing with him. The guy was flirting with me. No doubt. And it made me feel special, wanted. I hadn't felt that way in a long time. *What about Max*? My unhelpful brain supplied that thought, and I ignored it.

I appreciated my family and Amica, but I missed the intimacy of being in a relationship. People often thought introverts wanted to be by themselves all the time. And while that was true to some extent—my energy came from being alone, being able to process my thoughts—I still craved that intimacy, connections with other people. When had I gotten so lonely?

"Tell me what you're thinking."

"No."

She touched my hand and then tilted my face up and brushed back my hair. "Come on, little bro," she said. "Tell your big sis all about it."

I smiled at that. "It was only four minutes." She shrugged but didn't back down.

"I had this call from a customer. And it was weird and wonderful all at the same time."

"Really? That sounds interesting."

"He was flirting with me, and he had this husky voice. It seemed to get deeper the more I talked to him and he had this laugh." I shook my head. What did it matter anyway?

"And it made you feel..." she prompted.

"Yes," I said. "Exactly. It made me feel."

She pulled me into a hug. I tried to blink away my tears, but it was no use.

"When did I stop feeling?"

"You were just protecting yourself, Chase." She pulled away, tucking my hair behind my ears. She reached for my sunglasses and handed them to me to put on. "But you don't need protection anymore. You've got this."

"Possibly."

"Are you going to go out with him?"

"Who? Max?"

"No, the customer."

I stared at her in shock. Was she crazy? "I can't go out with a customer. It's unethical. And I could lose my job."

"Details."

"I do think it's time to put myself back out there. I don't want to be alone all my life."

She hugged me again and kissed my forehead like I was one of her kids.

"You're right," she said. "And you might get hurt again, but it's worth it, Chase. So worth it, when you find the person you're meant to be with."

"What if I don't believe in that soul mate, happily ever after, crap?"

"Well, then just find that guy who makes you happy for right now. But you can't fool me. I know you believe in all that crap. Cameron just wasn't the right guy for you."

"I'm not sure Max is either," I said. I wasn't sure what to do.

"Well, you'll never know unless you try." She winked at me, before getting up and jumping into the pool, splashing around with her husband and her babies.

That was what I wanted. A family of my own. A person of my own. Maybe I should give Max another chance. Just based on the fact that I couldn't stop thinking about him this whole week and the only time he was out of my thoughts was when the guy on the phone flirted with me. I just wouldn't let things go as far as they did with Cameron. The first sign that Max couldn't deal with my anxiety, that he wanted me to be someone else other than who I was, it would be over.

And that was probably what I was afraid of most. What if I got further in and Max showed his true colors? Would I be able to recover from that? I shook those thoughts away. That kind of thinking is why I was still alone after two years. I was going to take a chance on Max. I had a feeling that maybe, just maybe, Max was worth it.

Taking that first step wasn't as easy as I thought it would be. Mostly because Max gave up trying to talk to me. While I appreciated his restraint, his acknowledgment of my wishes, it made everything harder. Because now I had to be the one to initiate contact. Talking to people, even those I wanted to talk to, was not my strong suit. I was already nervous. What if Max decided he just couldn't deal with the ups and downs of my moods? What if he was no longer interested? As I entered the lunchroom, I saw Max getting up to leave. My call had run late, right through the lunch hour. I was thankful that I could even squeeze it in before two o'clock. Sometimes that happened and my blood sugar went a little low. I kept snacks in my desk just for those occasions.

As Max approached me, I wasn't sure he was even going to look up at me. But at the last second as if he couldn't help himself, Max glanced up and I smiled at him.

"Hello, Max," I said as we were passing each other.

His mouth fell wide open and he stumbled. After he was already past me, he said, "Hey, Chase." I resisted the urge to watch him walk out of the lunchroom.

There weren't many people still eating. The few people I did have lunch with had already gone. I didn't mind eating by myself. It gave me time to think about Max and the startled look on his face. We had another planning meeting this afternoon, and I couldn't wait.

When I entered the room for the meeting, Max and Jon were already sitting together talking. I flexed my hands. It was time for me to be brave. I took a deep breath, encouraged by the smile Max gave me when he saw me. I lifted my hand in greeting and made my way over to the pair.

"Hey, Jon?" I said. "Do you mind if I team up with Max today? I have a few ideas I want to run by him."

"No, that's fine."

At that moment, Amica walked in.

"There's my new partner," he said as he made his way over to her. She glanced at him and then at us and smiled. She waved before taking a seat.

Now that we were basically alone, it was awkward.

"I um..." Max started and then cleared his throat.

I sat down beside him and smiled patiently, letting him take whatever time he needed to get out whatever it was he wanted to say. He seemed to debate with himself for a moment and then he said, "I'm sorry, Chase."

"I appreciate that Max." I bit my lip for a second, thinking. "What are you sorry for?"

Max closed his eyes as if dreading the question. When he opened them again, he shook his head. "Honestly? I don't know. But something I did or something I said bothered you, and I never wanted to bother you or hurt you so I'm sorry that it did." He finished, rolling his eyes at his stuttering.

I laughed. "It's okay, Max. Honestly, I think I overreacted. A bit. Maybe."

"Can I ask...?"

"Please don't. Let's just start over." I held out my hand. "Hi. I'm Chase. I'm a Pisces. And I get nervous when I talk to other people."

Max shook my hand, a smile on his face. "Hi. I'm Max," he said. "I love people. I'm a bit loud, I can be very competitive, and I think about you all the time."

My breath caught in my throat. Max thought about me?

"I'm sorry, that was too soon. I don't know why I said that. It's true, though. It seems like all I'm going to do is keep apologizing, so I might as well establish right now that I fuck up. A lot. I try not to, but it just happens."

The man was charming as hell, and I wanted to just eat him up. This was probably going to end badly. Getting hurt seemed to be inevitable and yet at that moment with Max smiling at me and still holding my hand, the electricity sizzling between us, I wasn't sure I cared.

"I think I need my hand back," I said.

"Of course. I'm sorry."

I laughed again. "You don't have to keep apologizing. It's just that Ben is watching us, and inter-office fraternization is frowned upon."

"Is that what we're doing?" Max asked. "Fraternizing?" He released my hand, but his fingers brushed against mine softly.

The gesture was so intimate, erotic, that I had to shift in my seat. Thankfully, there was a table between us.

"Everything all right here, guys?" Ben came over to personally handle the situation. At least, we were no longer shaking hands.

"Yes, it's fine." I smiled up at my supervisor. "We were just talking about the positive and negatives of mentoring during a call versus role-playing. Max was telling me that statistics show that people learn in different ways and some people are visual learners, some people are auditory learners, and some are kinesthetic learners."

"So, we really need to tailor our mentoring program towards each individual," Max finished.

Years and years of getting away with stuff must've been the reason Max was able to keep his cool. At least, that was what I assumed.

"Okay, it sounds like you guys have it under control. I'll leave you to it."

"Wow that was some quick thinking," Max said.

"I'm quick on my feet."

"Only your feet?"

I did not take the bait. I was already having a hard time concentrating with my body reacting to Max being so near. "Let's just get to work."

"Yes, before Ben thinks we need to be separated."

I almost giggled at that. I was never the troublemaker, but I had to admit, it felt good.

We worked on the project for the next hour and a half. Max had a lot of good ideas. He was very intelligent, and we worked well together. Even if we did nothing more than this, it was worth it. But I wanted more. So much more.

As we left the meeting, Max checked that no one, especially Ben, was paying attention. He then grabbed my hand and pulled me into a supply closet nearby.

"Are we going to make out?" I asked before I could think about it. I had no idea why I said it. I certainly wasn't making a suggestion. It was too soon for that.

"What? No. I mean unless you want to..."

"Then what's on your mind, Max?"

"Oh, I, well..." He looked down, rubbing the back of his neck. This nervous side of him was very attractive. What happened to that confident guy from just a few weeks ago?

Max took a deep breath. "I'm messing this up so much," he said, shaking his head. He looked up at me, his gaze intent. "Have dinner with me tonight?"

Max was still holding my hand. The intimacy of the touch made it hard to breathe. I imagined what it would be like to do more, to be more with Max. I had to shut down those thoughts. Max waited for my answer, his face already falling like he knew my answer.

"Yes, Max," I said. "I would love to."

"Great!" His face lit up and I wanted to always be the one to put that smile there. "How about if I pick you up at seven? You think about where you want to go."

I pulled my hand free and his smile faltered. I grinned at him as I reached in my bag to pull out my gel pen. Taking his hand again, I wrote my address on his arm.

"See you then," I said. As I walked out, excitement zipped through me. It was an unusual and addictive feeling. It wasn't until I reached my desk that I remembered I would have to decide on dinner. Decisions made me crazy. What if I picked the wrong thing? What if I picked something Max didn't want to do? Were we going to a nice place or somewhere casual? This would haunt me the rest of the day.

Then I remembered the feel of Max's hand in mine. His eyes watching me as if I was the most important one in the room. The smile on his face and his adorable nervousness. And I thought about how I really, really wanted to kiss him.

ELEVEN

Max

MY CONCENTRATION AT WORK WAS SHOT. The thought of spending time with Chase had my pulse racing, but the fear that I would once again fuck this up kept my stomach in knots. If I knew what happened the first time, it would have eased my mind. I would just not do it again. My customers definitely didn't get the service they deserved, but I couldn't find the strength to care. At one point, Dylan rolled his chair over and took ahold of my arm, which I'd been staring at for the last ten minutes. He read the address written in Chase's sloppy writing and shook his head.

"I'm worried about you," he said.

'Why? It's just dinner. I can handle it."

"I've never seen you like this, Max. If this goes wrong, you'll be devastated."

"What makes you say that? And I'm offended you think I'll mess this up."

"A—you've been moping for the last two weeks after a work meeting went wrong." He held up his hands counting off his points. I didn't mention the fact that he was mixing his letters and numbers. "And B," he said, holding up his second finger. "You're not the one I'm worrying about."

That made me even more nervous. Did he think Chase would do something? What if this was an elaborate plan of Chase's to get revenge. Okay, that was ridiculous.

"What do you mean?"

"Being in a relationship with someone with anxiety can be challenging. You have to understand how best to help them and realize that sometimes there is absolutely nothing you can do."

"I know." I sometimes forgot that Sadie suffered from anxiety. It didn't usually affect anything we did together because she was more comfortable around me, and if she was worried about something, she wouldn't necessarily say anything to me.

"No. You don't know, Max. Not unless you live it."

"It's only dinner."

"We both know that's not true. And if it is, then you should just cancel. Chase isn't a casual type of guy, Max. You're either in it or you aren't."

"I'm in."

"I had no doubt." He smiled briefly. "Sometimes things just don't work out. I don't want to see Chase hurt. But I don't want to see you hurt, either."

"I've got this."

But he had reason to be concerned. I'd been a mess these last few weeks with Chase refusing to talk to me. Getting to know him, really getting to know him, and then losing him, might be devastating.

I had no idea where Chase would want to eat, but I wanted to look good for him. Show him I was serious about this. About us. Throughout the drive to his place, I used calming techniques I'd learned from Dylan. If I was a nervous wreck, it would spike Chase's anxiety. But I wouldn't be able to contain my excitement at being on a date with him. It was a date, right? I wasn't going to worry about that right now. I'd let Chase set the pace.

I picked him up at his apartment. I'd texted him to let him know what time I'd be there. He was waiting out front. I figured he didn't want the awkwardness of having me in his apartment. Hell, I was surprised he let me pick him up. I thought he'd want to have his own vehicle.

"Hey, Max," Chase said, his voice slightly breathless. "You look nice."

"So do you," I said, smiling at him. It was an understatement. The man was gorgeous in a blue-green shirt, which brought out the blue in his eyes, and tapered black pants and his black boots. He was sexy as hell, and I wanted to take him home and ravish him. Too soon for that. I should really find out if it was a date first. "Where to?"

Chase's smile faltered. He swallowed and looked away. "I'm not sure..."

"I have a couple of ideas," I said, glad I was prepared. Dylan had mentioned making decisions was not always an easy thing to do when you had anxiety. I named off three places I thought Chase would like.

He smiled gratefully. "I love Italian food so I'm good with Santinos off of Third Street. I've heard they have good food."

"Perfect." I started the car and we headed into the traffic. Rush hour had almost passed, but it was still busy. I was disappointed I couldn't stare at him like I wanted to do. When I did glance at him, he was either staring forward with a grin on his face or watching me. I winked at him at one point and his cheeks pinkened. I loved that his skin was so responsive. It gave me ideas I didn't need sitting this close to him.

We chatted about work a little, and Chase talked about his nieces and their dance recital this coming weekend. His voice was full of love for them and it did things to my heart.

At the restaurant, he struggled over what to order. I gave him plenty of time. I told him a few of my favorite dishes. He finally ordered the manicotti, and I ordered shrimp alfredo. I asked him a head of time if he had any allergies. I really wanted to kiss him later if I got the chance, and I didn't want something like allergies to get in the way.

"I'm sorry," Chase said after we ordered. "I have anxiety. I'm sure you already know that. It's frustrating, but it's not going away so..." He shrugged.

The moment felt important, like Chase put it out there to see how I'd react. To give me a chance to back out now. "I know someone with anxiety, so I have some experience with it," I said, hoping that was the right thing to say.

"Toby?" Chase said quietly.

I laughed. How did he know I had a dog? "Yeah, you're right, Toby does have anxiety. But I was actually talking about Sadie, Dylan's girlfriend."

"Does she have generalized anxiety?"

"I think it's more of a social anxiety. She really doesn't like crowds. I've learned a lot from just being around her."

My phone rang and I knew who it was before I even looked at the screen. I sighed and gave Chase an apologetic smile.

"Hello, Janice." I could have recited her words verbatim. It was always the same. Toby heard footsteps and was freaking out. I'd given him an anxiety pill before I'd left. "Put him on," I said. "Toby would you please just chill? No one's out to hurt you." Nothing I said made a difference. I ended the call and glanced over at Chase. I didn't want to end our evening, but I needed to take care of Toby. Chase was quiet, and it reminded me of the last time I had to leave him. That was also after a call about Toby. Maybe Chase didn't like the fact that our time was being interrupted. He didn't seem like he was that self-centered. But what else could it be? Did he think he wasn't important to me? Which was utterly ridiculous.

"Chase would you mind if we got our food to go? I have something I need to take care of at home."

"Sure." Chase looked even more upset as he avoided looking at me.

I immediately realized my mistake. "Let me be clear," I said. "I don't want our time to end, but there's something I have to take care of, and I was hoping you would go with me."

"You want me to go with you to your home?"

"Yes, I know that might be weird for you and if you're uncomfortable at all..."

"No, it's fine, Max. I'd love to go home with you." He blushed at that. "I mean..."

I laughed again, taking his hand. "I know what you mean. And if you want to leave at any point just let me know, and I'll take you home."

We drove back to my apartment. I'd been upset with Toby for messing up my date, but now Chase was going to be in my home. I'd have to give Toby an extra treat.

As soon as we opened the door, Toby rushed over to Chase, barking at him like the man was a serial killer. I shook my head. Crazy dog.

"Toby, stop. This is Chase. He's a friend."

Chase leaned down, letting the dog sniff his hand. Toby stopped barking, and I picked him up, scratching his head.

"Toby is a dog." Chase stared at me as if reassessing everything he knew.

"Of course. What did you think?"

"Never mind," he said. "It doesn't matter."

I thought back to the first night I'd had to leave Chase and then tonight.

"You thought I was talking to a person? Someone with anxiety?" The things I'd said to Toby...no wonder he didn't want anything to do with me. God, I was an idiot. "My neighbor calls me anytime Toby gets anxious. Usually we have this structure to our day. I go to work and come home. If I break that routine, it upsets him. He starts freaking out, and my neighbor comes over and calls me. She holds the phone up to the door so he can hear my voice. It doesn't really matter what I say to him. Just hearing my voice helps him. Still, some of the things I said were insensitive. I'm sorry, Chase. No wonder you hated me."

"I didn't hate you." He scratched behind Toby's ears, not looking at me, as he took a deep breath. "I had a boyfriend who didn't always do well with anxiety."

"How long were you together?"

"Two years."

"That's a long time. Can I ask why you guys broke up? Did he cheat on you?"

"I wish."

"You wish your boyfriend had cheated on you?"

"It would be easier to explain, I guess." He shrugged, as he glanced up at me. "I don't really want to talk about this anymore."

I put Toby down and held up the to-go boxes. "Are you hungry?"

"Starving," he said with a laugh.

"Want to watch a movie while we eat?"

"Sure. But why don't you choose? I'm decided out."

I gave Toby some food so he wouldn't bother us. We ate while we watched a comedy that was just released. I definitely picked the right movie because I loved listening to Chase laugh. He didn't laugh often enough, and I knew in that moment, I would do everything I could to get him to laugh more.

After the movie, we talked about our families while Toby lounged between us.

"You have five siblings?" Chase stared at me, his eyes narrowed. "Really?"

"Why is that surprising?"

His face turned red. "I thought you were an only child."

I didn't know whether to laugh or be insulted.

Chase smiled sweetly. "You're so sure of yourself all the time."

"Are you sure you don't mean loud and obnoxious?"

"That too," Chase said with a laugh. His smile really did light up his whole face. And those dimples.

"I'm the second child in a large family. The only way to get attention is to be loud and obnoxious. Plus, I was the comedian of the family. Always playing pranks."

"That, I believe." Chase looked at me, biting his lip. "Can I ask you something?"

"Of course."

But he still hesitated. "Are you bi?"

Of all the things I thought he'd ask, that wasn't even close to being on the list. "No. Definitely not."

"Oh, okay. I'm sorry," Chase said, frowning.

"What are you sorry about?" I reached over to touch his arm, but he pulled his hand away.

"I thought maybe this was a date."

"That's what I was hoping. Do you not want it to be a date?"

"No, I mean, yes. But you said you're not bi."

"I'm not. I'm gay."

Chase looked even more confused, if that's possible, but I didn't get it.

"I really like guys," I said, wanting to be clear. How was this even a question?

"I know what you mean." He laughed nervously. "But

when we first met, you thought I was a woman and you hit on me."

"No. I didn't."

"You said and I quote, 'Hey beautiful, I'd like some of that.'" He quirked his eyebrow up at me in challenge.

"That part is true," I said. "But I did not think you were a girl."

"I saw your face when I turned around, Max. You were shocked." He sat up straighter on the couch, his blue eyes flashing.

"I wasn't shocked that you were male. You have an amazing ass that had to belong to a guy. I was shocked because..." I hesitated. I didn't want to piss him off, but I needed to be honest with him. "You had this look of pure loathing on your face. So, I acted like it was a mistake. You clearly did not want me hitting on you."

"I'm sorry," Chase said. "You'd be surprised at how many people mistake me for a woman because of my hair. I thought about cutting it but..."

"No, don't do that."

Chase smiled. "You like my hair?"

"Yes, very much." I'd fantasized about that hair, but I wasn't about to tell him how I wanted to wrap my hand around it and pull him closer.

"Tell me more."

"I'm trying to be good here."

"What does that mean exactly?"

"I know you have boundaries. You like your space, and I just want take it slow."

"You're going too slow, Max. I'm not made of glass. I won't break. If you're worried about doing something I don't like then, just ask first."

"It's that easy?"

"It can be," Chase said. "Or I can just take the initiative."

He leaned closer, mere inches from my lips. I wanted to close the gap between us, but I needed him to be the one to do it. He bit his lip, before leaning in to touch our lips together. The kiss was shy at first, and then he grew bolder. I let Chase set the pace, and when he opened his mouth to me, I couldn't hold back anymore. I pulled him closer, exploring his mouth as our tongues twisted together. I wrapped my hand in his hair, that glorious hair, and pulled him closer still.

Chase moaned and it went straight to my cock. I pulled back. "Chase," I said, trying to catch my breath. "We should take it slow."

"Stop talking, Max." He straddled my body, rubbing our cocks together.

"You're making this hard."

"That was my intent."

I needed to stop this. I didn't want Chase regretting anything. But more than that, every encounter I'd had with a guy had ended after sex. Maybe it lasted for a week of sex, but it still ended. I grew bored. I was sure that wouldn't happen with Chase. Positive. But I had something to prove. Not to him. To myself. I could do this. Have a relationship that wasn't just about sex.

I pushed against his chest. Chase looked dazed. His pupils blown and his lips swollen. I almost gave in right then. "We need to stop."

TWELVE
Chase

MY BODY BURNED WITH DESIRE. I wanted Max, like yesterday, and yet he was pushing me away. I'd been too bold. I wasn't usually like that, but he'd been going so slow, and I felt safe with Max. I let him drive me to the restaurant. Something I would normally never do. Max had been so sweet at the beginning of our date. He knew I had issues with making decisions, and instead of making a big deal of it, he gave me time to make up my mind, even narrowing the choices for me. It wasn't that I didn't know what I wanted, I was just nervous about making the wrong choice and ruining the whole evening. It was too much pressure. But Max was so understanding.

It almost went sideways when Max got the call about Toby. Why did I assume he was talking to someone like that? I heard the dog barking in the background, but I didn't put it all together.

And then I'd questioned his sexuality. It felt like a date, but I'd panicked. What if I was wrong? But I hadn't been wrong. Kissing and touching Max had set me on fire, and I wanted so much more. The press of his cock against mine almost drove me over the edge.

Only to get pushed aside. I was not giving up that easily.

"I want you, Max," I said, slipping my hand between the gap in his shirt buttons to touch his warm skin. I undid another button to give me better access. I could see the outline of his nipple on his shirt and that was my target. I rubbed my thumb over the peak, and he arched his back, pushing his straining cock against me.

"Chase," he moaned. "You're killing me."

I kissed him again, and Max pulled back. Again.

"We need to slow down. I don't want you to regret this."

"I don't want to go slow, Max." I said, getting frustrated. "I know what I want."

"It's not you. It's me," he said.

"Are we breaking up already?" I moved off of him so I could focus on his words and not his muscled legs and straining erection.

"No. Poor choice of words. You're not just some guy to me, Chase. You're important to me." He waved his hand between the two of us. "This is important to me."

I knew the last part of his statement was what I should focus on, but I couldn't get past the first part. I wasn't just some guy. It reminded me that Max had been with many guys. I wasn't that experienced. And after Cameron always wanting me to bottom, because he had to be the one in control, I wanted to top. To slide into Max's body, giving him pleasure. But what if that wasn't what he wanted. How could I be so stupid as to think I could even compete with all those other guys?

"Where did you go?" Max asked, tilting my face toward him.

I wanted to hide from his gaze, to retreat back into my

shell, but where had that gotten me? "I don't have much experience. I know you've been with a lot of—"

"Stop," he said. "You are the only one I want, Chase. And you're worth waiting for."

It was sweet that Max wanted to take it slow. Frustrating as hell, but sweet. "We can still make out, though, right?"

"Oh, yeah," Max said, pulling me into a lingering kiss. "We can still make out."

I loved my job, but this was the first time I'd been really excited to go to work. I couldn't wait to see Max again. We couldn't be open about our relationship at work, but there were plenty of lingering looks and secret touches.

I hated the elevator. Too many people pressed together. I usually got to work early so there were fewer people there. If I was running late, I took the stairs. Max and I met at the elevator this morning. Unfortunately, there were others around, but for once I didn't notice the mingled smells of perfume, deodorant, and body odor that seemed to permeate the small space. Max distracted me by lightly sliding our fingers together. I wanted to slam him against the back of the elevator and climb his body. I squeezed his fingers to stop their motion. It was too much. I didn't need to leave the elevator sporting an erection.

My body temperature was set to overheated for the rest of the day. If it had been winter, I could have worn a sweater to hide the bulge in my pants. Damn the summer months. Max teased me all morning, and I'd finally had enough. Around midmorning, I dropped a note onto Max's desk and made my way to the copy room. He'd been on a call, so I wasn't sure he'd be able to follow. I waited by the copier, pretending to make copies. Max arrived shortly after, shutting the door. I pulled him into a kiss.

"I don't think I solved that guy's problem," he said between kisses.

"Shut up and solve mine." I pushed him against the copy machine, grinding my cock against his.

We made out like teenagers for a few moments, and then I put some distance between us. I needed to get control before I walked back out there.

"Missed you," Max said, and my heart melted. The guy could be so sweet.

"Missed you, too."

"See you at lunch?" His voice was hesitant as if he was afraid I wouldn't sit with him.

"Absolutely." I winked at him before sliding out the door. If my calls didn't go long so I could keep that promise.

I had a few slow moments with no calls. It didn't happen often, but there were slow days. I thought about Max. Sneaking around was exciting, but office romances were strictly forbidden. Too much drama. I needed to keep my job, but I couldn't resist Max.

"Hello, boys," I said, sitting down next to Max and Dylan at a table in the lunchroom. Dylan glanced quickly at Max, but otherwise hid his surprise well.

"How's it going, Chase?" he said.

"Very well, thank you." I didn't know what to say. That wasn't my forte and Max, who was the master at carrying a conversation, was strangely silent. He studied his sandwich and then looked up and our eyes locked.

"Should I leave you guys alone?" Dylan asked. The snark in his voice told me that was the last thing he was going to do.

"Shut up." Max flushed. I wasn't sure I'd ever seen him embarrassed.

We chatted for a few minutes, mostly complaining about customers who didn't understand technology, and I tried not to stare at Max. Enough people would be curious about why I was sitting with them. I didn't need to throw fuel on their speculation.

"I'm going to get a soda. Do you guys want anything?"

"I'll go with you," I said.

Dylan opened his mouth to say something, but nothing came out. He shook his head. Whether it was to deny he wanted anything or because we caught him off guard, I didn't know.

Max turned the lights on in the small room, and I turned them back off, kissing him for several long moments. When had I become so bold? I switched the light back on and reached for a soda from the small dorm fridge. Even though the lights were on and anyone could've walked in, Max grabbed my ass when I bent over.

"Sorry, couldn't help myself," he said with a smile. Why were there so many people at work? I couldn't wait to be alone with him.

We deposited our money and restocked the fridge.

The rest of the day, we found little moments to be together, and I could barely keep the smile from my face. My coworkers stared at me like they'd never seen me before. Gina asked me if I was okay more than once. At one point, she stopped by my desk to ask if I was on new medication and if so, she wanted to try it. I just grinned at her like an idiot.

Amica caught me in the hall at last break. I hadn't seen Max, so he was probably on a call.

"So, you and Max." she said. "Spill."

"I don't know what you're talking about."

"Right. Any idea why the lights in the snack room keep going off with people in there?"

Before I could deny it again, she leaned in closer.

"Come on, Chase. Let me live vicariously through you. I haven't had a date in forever."

I looked around to make sure no one was listening. Then I zipped my lips, indicating it was a secret. She mimicked my motions and threw away the key.

"We went on a date last night," I said. I enjoyed having someone to confide in. I missed things like this. Having friends. The excitement of having a crush. Being able to touch someone. Kiss someone. It was a heady experience and I loved every minute of it.

"And by the look on both your faces it went well."

I nodded. "I have to get back."

Amica squeezed my arm. "I'm happy for you, Chase," she said. "But I want details. Call me tonight."

I promised I would and went back to my desk. My life had changed so much in the last few weeks, and it was all because of Max.

THIRTEEN

Max

DYLAN ROLLED HIS CHAIR OVER, almost hitting me in the process. "Dude, what's going on with you and Corrigan?"

"What do you mean?" Throughout the week, Chase and I had flirted at work and then hung out together at my place. Mostly that was because of Toby's anxiety, but I did wonder if Chase didn't want me to see his place. We'd made out a lot. I stopped it from going much further. I wanted to take it slow. It had been one of the best weeks of my life, and I was surprised that Dylan hadn't cornered me before now.

"Your goal was to beat him at the number one spot for customer service rep, and now you guys are best buds."

I shrugged, typing on my computer, finishing the notes from the last call.

"Is he your boyfriend?"

"We haven't really talked about it," I said.

"You hang out together all the time."

"I don't want to scare him off, okay. No sense in labeling it."

"So, you're not hooking up with other guys?"

I stared at him. "Of course not." I couldn't believe he'd say that. I thought we were friends.

"Heck yeah, you guys are going steady."

I pushed his chest, so his chair rolled away.

Dylan laughed. "Speaking of hanging out. We still on for tonight?" It was our standard video game night.

"About that," I said, not looking at him. "I thought about inviting Chase."

"Seriously? You can't go one night without him?"

"Isn't your girlfriend there every time?"

"First of all, she's a gamer and much better than you and I put together. Second of all, we don't even know if Chase can play."

"Chase can play."

"Third of all," he said as if I hadn't interrupted him. "She's my girlfriend, so you just made my point for me. Chase is your boyfriend."

"Just don't tell him that."

"I'm happy for you, Max. I just worry."

"You're like a mother hen."

"That boy is going to stomp on you with his size ten boots."

The analogy made me laugh. Chase was fierce and I wouldn't want to be on his bad side—again. "It might be fun."

"Heck yeah. I'm looking forward to it."

"Hey."

"The man-killer Maxwell Sloan, getting his heart handed to him. I've been waiting for this moment."

"Shut up."

"Heck off."

"That's really not a thing."

"It's catching on."

"It's really not."

The light on Dylan's phone lit up. "Bring the boy," he said, rolling back to his desk.

"He's the same age as you," I said, but he ignored me.

At first I'd been worried about Toby getting used to Chase. He didn't really do well with new people. It had helped that we stayed at my house all week. I needn't have worried. Toby seemed as enamored of Chase as I was. He curled up in Chase's lap the moment he sat on the couch.

"Hey, cutie," he said, stroking his ears. "Love the hoodie." Toby had on a blue Adidog hoodie. "But why do you put a shirt on him during the summer?"

"He licks and scratches himself when he's nervous. He has a few sore spots. This is the only way to keep him from making it worse."

"Poor baby." Chase nuzzled him, and I was suddenly jealous of my dog.

"How about me?" I asked, sitting beside him.

"Are you feeling neglected?" He leaned into me.

"Yes," I said softly as he trailed kisses along my jaw. I growled at his teasing and pulled him in for a kiss. Toby jumped down as I pulled Chase on top of me. Toby needed to learn sooner than later, that Chase was all mine.

We kissed for a while until things started to get heated. "We need to finish getting ready. They'll be here soon."

Chase sighed as he sat up.

I understood his frustration. I wanted him. Like crazy. But our relationship was so new. It was like the game of Jenga. If you moved any one piece the whole thing could come tumbling down. Our relationship was fragile. That one shift could cause the whole thing to fall apart. Chase didn't understand, and sometimes I had to work hard at convincing him I wanted him without letting it get too far.

Adding Chase to my nights with Dylan and Sadie was another thing that could topple us. I wasn't used to the whole relationship thing. What if I sucked at it? Then Chase would leave me.

"I'm the one who should be nervous," Chase said.

"What do you mean?" Was I that obvious?

"You bite your thumb when you're nervous."

I put my hand down. I hadn't even noticed.

"Come on," he said, pulling me up. "Let's finish getting ready."

There wasn't much left to do. I made queso dip and Chase scrubbed the countertops. I told him I'd already cleaned, but it seemed to help calm him down. He also made chocolate chip cookies. It was the perfect dessert to go with pizza and beer. Dylan and Sadie were picking up the pizza on their way over.

"Is there anything else I can do?" Chase glanced around the room, but there was nothing to do but wait.

"I can think of one thing you can do."

"Really? What is it?" He seemed so eager. I wrapped my arms around his waist and pulled him close.

"Help me calm down?" I kissed Chase's neck, finding my favorite spot under his ear. His breath caught.

"This is calming you down?"

"Not all of me," I said, pressing my erection against him.

Chase laughed. "You're such a tease, Maxwell. Don't cock that thing, if you don't plan on shooting it."

"I blame you for looking so damn hot."

"You say the sweetest things."

I wrapped my hands in the long blond strands of his hair, pulling to expose the long line of his neck. I licked the pulse there, and he gasped.

"Max." He moaned, rubbing against me.

"Maybe I should call Dylan and cancel the whole thing."

"I want to make a good impression, Max."

"You are making a good impression." I squeezed his ass. And he shuddered.

Chase sighed and pushed me away. "I'll get the fruit salad out of the fridge. It should be cold enough."

I kissed his cheek. "Fine. I'll be good."

It was a good thing we put some distance between us because Dylan and Sadie arrived not long after, pizza in hand.

"Yay," I said. "The pizza's here. I mean the guests are here."

Sadie smacked my arm and gave me a playful kiss on the cheek. "You mean your competition is here."

"I definitely mean that."

Chase shifted on his feet as he watched us and waited for me to make introductions. Of course, he knew Dylan, especially since Chase had been sitting with us quite a bit more at lunch, but this was his first time meeting Dylan's girlfriend.

"Chase, this is Sadie, Dylan's best half..." I realized we should have talked about what labels we were using. Did I introduce him as my boyfriend? Friend didn't seem right. "Sadie, this is Chase." Since I didn't know what to call him, I figured I might as well stake my claim with actions instead of words. I wrapped my arm around him.

Chase didn't seem to mind. He hugged me back, using his free hand to shake theirs. "Nice to meet you."

"Oh, it's very nice meeting you." Sadie winked at me.

There was no way this evening was going to go well. No way at all.

But I was wrong. Chase loved video games, so he fit right in. He was very good at Gears of War, so Sadie had tougher competition than she was used to. She still won, of course, but she had to put a little more effort into it.

I sighed in relief as we finished the game and the pizza. I'd been worried Dylan and Sadie would tease me about the fact that Chase was the first guy I'd ever brought into the group. I didn't want to remind Chase I didn't usually do relationships, or at least I didn't do them very well. And I definitely didn't want to remind him I usually only did hookups. But my friends were being good for the most part. Toby was happy as could be since all his favorite people were in one room. I even noticed Dylan sneaking him pizza under the table earlier. Did he not know how that would end? I would be the one cleaning it up. Everyone seemed so happy I didn't say a word.

The night went very smooth until it was time for them to leave.

"It was a pleasure to meet you, Chase." Sadie gave him a hug. Yes, they had already gotten that close. Although I would have preferred she ask first, Chase didn't seem to mind.

"It was a pleasure to meet you, too."

Dylan shook Chase's hand. "Glad we all could hang out," Dylan said. "This is the first time Max has ever invited someone to join us."

I shook my head at Dylan. He needed to stop speaking immediately.

"Really?" Chase turned to look at me, and I abruptly stopped and smiled.

"Oh, yeah. He doesn't usually have boyfriends. Just hookups."

Everyone stared at Dylan like he was an idiot. Which he was.

"Is that so?" Chase looked at me again.

Sadie slapped Dylan on the arm. "I think it's time for us go before you screw up anything else."

After they left, I started cleaning up. I usually left it until morning, but I needed something to do other than see the disappointment on Chase's face. I should have talked to Dylan ahead of time, but I'd been afraid of putting the idea in his head.

"I think everyone had a good time," I said as I threw away the plates and started washing the glasses. There weren't many. I wished there was more, so I'd have more to do. I started wiping the counter when Chase's hand covered mine.

"We should talk about this."

"About what?"

"About whatever is bothering you, Max."

I turned to face him. I didn't see the disappointment or anger I expected, only concern.

"Remember this is my way of dealing with stress." He took the cloth from my hand and finished cleaning the counter. We both washed our hands, and Chase guided me to the couch. "Talk to me."

"I haven't been in many relationships," I said. "The ones I have been in were mostly about sex. I just don't want you to think that I'm that guy. That I'm only interested in one thing."

Chase laughed. "Seriously?"

"I pour my heart out to you, and you laugh?"

"I'm sorry for laughing, Max, I really am. But I have been trying to have sex with you for the last week, so no, I don't think that's the only thing you're after, or we probably would have done it by now."

I laughed. "Good point."

"I can see you're really trying, and it makes me feel special. I get that you have a past. I have one, too. Although I suspect it's not as active as yours." He sighed. "But maybe just as embarrassing."

"What do you mean?" I took his hand, trying to reassure him.

"I was in a serious relationship with a guy. We were together two years."

"This is the guy you wished had cheated on you?"

"No, I mean yes, but no. What happened was humiliating."

"Tell me." I squeezed his hand.

"He never took my anxiety seriously. He thought I should have been able to control it."

"Jerk," I muttered. His hair hid some of his face, but I could see a small smile on his lips at my comment.

"We went to the movies, and he bought the tickets online. I think that's the part that bothered me the most. He picked the seats, and they were right in the middle of the row. I just couldn't do it. I couldn't." He shook his head again.

I knew it was hard for him to admit. I lifted his chin, so he had to look at me. Tears shone in his eyes.

"It's stupid, I know."

"It's not," I said. "You're not comfortable sitting next to someone you don't know. In a dark theater." Something your boyfriend should know. But I didn't add that part. "What happened?"

He ducked his head again. "I think if he'd just acknowledged how hard it was for me, maybe I could've done it. Just sat there and tried to enjoy the movie. Lord knows I've done it before. He was angry. He told me I always ruined everything."

I pulled him closer, my grip tightening on his hand. I was furious. How could someone treat him like that? Someone who supposedly loved him.

"He was yelling at me and everyone stared. I left the theater and him."

"He's an asshole."

Chase looked up at me, his eyes wide. "You don't think I overreacted?"

I cupped his face with my hands. "Listen to me, Chase. This was not your fault. You guys were dating for two years, right?"

He nodded.

"He must've known how uncomfortable this would be for you. How hard this would be for you. And not only did he pick seats that he knew you wouldn't like, he didn't even care. And maybe those were the only seats left and maybe that was the only choice he had, but not telling you ahead of time? Not preparing you or giving you a choice? Dick move. Then he embarrassed you in public. The guy is an asshole. I'm so sorry he did that to you."

Without warning, Chase was in my lap, hugging me tightly. "I can't believe you understand."

"You should never accept anything less. Nothing is wrong with you, Chase," I said, hoping he was hearing me and believing it. "We all have our little quirks, our things. When you care about somebody, when you love somebody, you love all of them."

Chase kissed me, ending my rant. "I want you so much, Max." He stood up and reached out for my hand. "Please, take me to bed."

FOURTEEN

Chase

MY STOMACH TWISTED AS I WAITED for Max to respond. I wasn't exactly sure what he was worried about, but I needed him to trust me. Long seconds ticked away as I waited for his answer. He stood, towering over me, and picked me up. I squeaked in surprise.

"Let's go," he said, carrying me to his bedroom. "Toby, you stay here." Of course, that didn't work. He shut the bedroom door with his foot and deposited me on the bed. I couldn't help laughing. Toby barked for a few moments in protest but quickly gave up.

"Are you sure?" Max said. "We could binge watch *The Office* again."

"Tempting. But I'd rather binge on you."

Max stripped off his shirt before stretching his body over mine and kissing me sweetly. I wasn't sure how slow he planned on going, but I was having none of it. I didn't usually take charge but with Max, it looked like I'd have to.

I turned us over so I was on top. Watching his eyes, I slowly unbuttoned my shirt. If he wanted slow, I could give it to him. His eyes darkened as I slid my shirt off. His hands held on to my waist, and the strength in his long fingers made me hard. I unbuckled my belt and pulled it off. He licked his lips as I undid the button of my pants and slid the zipper down. His thumb slipped inside my pants, rubbing my cock through my underwear. I moaned. I wanted to be naked now, but I didn't want to pull away from his touch.

"You're so hard for me already, babe," he said, awe in his voice. He pulled my underwear down enough for my cock to spring free. His hand tightened around my erection and I almost lost it.

"Wait," I said, trying to still his hand. "Too soon." It had been a while for me, not counting those endless jerk-off sessions I'd had thinking about Max.

He moved his hands, stretching them behind him to grab the bars of his headboard. "You're the boss. Tell me what to do."

Fuck. He looked gorgeous like that, his muscles bulging and the dark patches of hair under his arms. I had to shut my eyes for a minute to get control of my body. I quickly undressed the rest of the way. Max watched me, his eyes going darker still. He had definite bulge in his pants. I rushed to pull them off along with his underwear. Max was sexy with clothes but stunning without. His body was all hard muscles with a spattering of dark hair. I suddenly felt unsure. We hadn't talked about anything. What if...

"Don't overthink it, Chase. Do whatever you want to do."

I straddled him, leaning in to kiss him. "Do you have a preference?" I asked.

"If you're not sure, we don't have to do everything."

"I know what I want."

"Fuck, that's sexy. I'm yours, babe."

I kissed down his chest, licking his nipples. I could taste

sweat and his salty skin. I kissed down his abs, giving special attention to the trail of dark hair that led to his cock. It was standing and ready for me. I licked the slit and sucked the tip into my mouth. Max moaned, his hips thrusting upward. I tried to hold them down as I took his cock into my mouth. I didn't stay there long, I had plans and I didn't want him to come yet. I kissed my way down, my hair twisting around his cock.

"Fuck," Max groaned.

Remembering his fascination with my hair, I wrapped the strands around his erection and stroked him. "Is this what you want?"

"Oh, God, Chase," he said. "I won't last..."

I didn't want him to come just yet. I tucked that information away for later and continued my journey. I nipped at the inside of his thigh and then worked my way down to his hole, licking and teasing him.

"Please," he whined, as he pushed back against my tongue.

"Supplies?" I wanted to be inside him, now. I hoped he was okay with that plan.

His eyes were shut tight, making me wonder just how close he'd been. He pointed to the nightstand before gripping the headboard again.

I grabbed the lube and condoms. His eyes were open now, watching me. I poured lube on my fingers. "You okay with this?" I wanted to be sure.

"God, yes," he said.

That was all the encouragement I needed. I pressed a finger against his hole, and it slid in easily. He bore down on my finger as I added another one, scissoring him open. "You feel so tight and amazing. I can't wait to be inside you."

He responded with a needy whimper. I put the condom on and lubed up, replacing my fingers with the tip of my cock.

There was only a slight resistance before I was able to push in. He was so tight, I had to close my eyes to keep from coming right there. The sight of his body taking my cock like it was made for it was too intense. Too real.

"Move, babe," he said. "Please."

I pulled out and pushed in again. We soon found a rhythm, and I knew I wouldn't last. It had been too long and the stimuli were overwhelming. The tightness of his ass, the visual of Max taking it all, the smell of his sweat. I couldn't last. I came with a shout. The world exploding around me.

Max was almost there. I wrapped my hair around his erection and stroked him with it. His whole body tightened and he came.

I climbed up his spent body to kiss him.

"Your hair." He frowned. "I messed it up."

I laughed at that. "It'll wash."

We took a shower, exploring each other's bodies, which ended in another round. Afterward, I snuggled up to Max. I wasn't sure if he wanted me to stay the night or not, but the hand around my stomach holding me in place, gave me my answer.

The next day we lounged around Max's apartment, playing with Toby, sharing stories, and having lots of sex. It was amazing. He was so attentive to my needs, and he never belittled me. I felt cherished. I could definitely get used to this.

Max suggested I stay the weekend, so we made a trip to my apartment to get my stuff. It felt momentous, like he just didn't want to let me go. I worried we were moving too quickly, but then Max would kiss my neck and the fear would go away, at least temporarily.

The excitement and fear coursed through me in equal measures. I actually had nightmares that Max screamed at me in public. It was irrational. The anger on Max's face when I told him about Cameron was enough to reassure me. And yet the fear of losing control of the situation, never seemed to go away.

But neither did the excitement. I always enjoyed this part of a new relationship. It was as if was Christmas every day. Everything was exciting. Everything seemed possible. And although the fear was there lingering in the background, reminding me not to get too excited, I couldn't keep the smile off my face. For the longest time, my worry was that Max didn't really care for me. That this was some cruel joke to get back at me. After all, Max could have anyone he wanted, male or female. People loved him. Why would he want me? We were complete opposites. Max loved being around people. He loved the excitement of the limelight. He charmed everyone he met.

I avoided people any chance I could. I certainly didn't like attention drawn to myself. I didn't want to stand out. It seemed almost incomprehensible we were together, and yet we were. One of the reasons I had been hesitant was because Max seemed resistant to us having sex, which didn't make any sense because if I knew one thing about Max, it was that he liked sex. After our weekend together, all those fears washed away. Max was a very attentive lover, and yet I had to stop those thoughts as I arrived at the elevator. I tried not to think of all the people stuffed into the elevator with me. It did take care of the little problem I had a few minutes ago.

As I walked in, I noticed Max coming from the lounge, a cup of coffee in his hand. That was the first thing I did in the morning. Got my coffee. As we passed each other, Max whispered, "Hey, beautiful." I didn't say anything, but I couldn't help the smile on my face as our fingers touched briefly. I could get used to starting every single day like this.

I poured myself a cup of coffee. Max had returned my Yoda mug, and I made my way to my cubicle to start the day.

The first call came in almost as soon as I sat down. It wasn't long before I was fixing Internet problems, equipment problems, and payment problems.

I didn't see Max again until lunch. Thankfully, he was the only one at the table when I sat down. I wanted to kiss him, but that was impossible with everyone there. We talked about work and how our days were going, but I couldn't stop thinking about our weekend together.

"Last night was amazing," I said, my face turning red.

"The whole weekend was." Max leaned in closer so no one could hear them. "I was worried you might regret it," he said. His eyes cast downward as if he was afraid of what I might say next.

"Never." I squeezed his hand gently before letting go again. Max looked up and our eyes met. "Never," I repeated.

"I'm having a hard time keeping my hands to myself." He brushed his hand down my arm.

His low voice stirred my cock. "You can't talk like that, Max. Or touch me like that." I should have stepped away, but I couldn't bring myself to do it. "Not when we can't do anything about it."

"There's always the storage room."

I was tempted to take him up on his suggestion, but it was too risky. "I really don't want to get caught."

"Can I see you tonight?"

I sighed. "I'm having dinner with my sister and her family."

"Maybe tomorrow?"

"Come with me," I said, before I could lose my nerve. It was probably too soon for us to do the meet the family thing, but I really wanted him to come. "I'd love for you to meet my sister."

Before he could reply, Amica walked over and sat down. "Hey, guys, what's up?"

I let Max take over the conversation. He was good at that. Before long, he and Amica were laughing about something that happened that morning. The discussion continued around me but I lost track of it.

Max never answered me. Did he not want to meet my sister? Or did he just not have a chance to respond? I glanced up at him. He was watching me intently. He winked before answering Amica's question.

Jon joined us and although these were my friends—I could believe that now—I probably wouldn't participate in the conversation. I was good one-on-one but add more people, and I was not comfortable speaking. Every once in a while, Max asked me a direct question, and it wasn't like he was trying to get me to speak, which was exactly what Cameron would've done, but more about him letting me know he was still thinking of me. I appreciated that.

I left early to go back to my desk, hoping Max would follow. He did but instead of going to his desk, he lightly touched my elbow, steering me toward the copy room. Once inside he shut the door and pressed himself up against me.

"Please let me know if this is not okay," Max began. "I know it's wrong to just accost you like this, but I had to touch you."

I waited for Max to kiss me and realized he needed an answer first. "Yes," I said breathlessly. "Please." We only had a few minutes.

Max pressed our palms together, rocking against me as he claimed my mouth in a searing kiss. I practically melted in his arms, kissing him back urgently. Max pulled back and I whimpered in response. I wanted more.

"I just want to give you an answer," he said.

I could not for the life of me remember what question I asked. "Please," I said instead.

"We have to go back to work, Chase."

"Fuck it."

"I like it when you talk dirty to me." He kissed me again and then pulled himself away. "My answer is yes."

I looked at him blankly, arousal making me stupid.

"On going to see your sister. But hell, afterwards there might be some time for more of this. Three minutes not near enough time." He took a deep breath, kissed my forehead, and walked out of the copy room, shutting the door behind him.

I took a moment to get myself together, before going back to my desk. I still had another four hours of work before I'd get to see Max again. The anxiety that had been simmering below the surface all afternoon bubbled to the top by the end of the day. I wanted Max to meet my family, but knowing my sister, no way was this going to go well.

I planned to pick up Max around five thirty. I questioned my decision to drive every mile until I reached his apartment building. What had I been thinking? I was a careful driver. More than necessary, according to Cameron. He'd always made me nervous and caused me to make mistakes. Cameron would sometimes ask me to pull over so he could drive. I tried to push him from my mind. He really was an asshole. Why had I stayed with him for so long? And even though Max wasn't like that, I worried about making mistakes.

Max stood waiting for me when I pulled up to his building. He looked amazing and his smile was warm and inviting. My stomach did somersaults, mostly from nerves, as Max got in the car and buckled up. I turned on my blinker and took my time moving into traffic, not even looking at Max.

"Hey, I'm the one who should be nervous," he said. "I'm meeting your family."

"Are you?" I glanced over at him. He looked away, nervously, and his hand tapped on the side of his leg. I reached over and squeezed his hand. "My sister's going to love you."

"You don't know that." Max laughed. "There are plenty of people who don't like me."

I brought his hand up and kissed it, giving another squeeze before letting go to focus on the road. "I find that hard to believe."

The ride to my sister's home went smoothly. Max didn't pay any attention to my driving as if he trusted me completely. It really boosted my confidence, especially after the way Cameron had treated me.

As we got closer, Max seemed to get more nervous. His knee jiggled up and down and at one point, I put my hand on it to calm him. Max put his hand over mine and squeezed it.

"If I blow this, and I mean completely blow it," Max said, "you're not going to dump me, are you?"

"I guess it depends..."

Max pinched my arm.

"Ow," I said with a laugh. "Of course not, sweetie. I'll still love you even if my sister doesn't."

I realized what I'd said as soon as I said it and wished I could take it back. How could I bring out the L word, even as a joke?

When I glanced at Max, he was smiling. "The way to a woman's heart is through her kids," he said. "Kids love me."

"We'll see." Sunny's kids could be a handful. It might be fun to watch Max squirm.

Once we arrived at the house, I realized I should've warned Max. My sister could be a little eccentric. I tried to see the house through Max's eyes. Her tastes were very eclectic. Her house was a hodgepodge of furniture and knickknacks. She liked what she liked, even if it didn't go together. Her only reoccurring theme was animals. An elephant coffee table, the glass top being held up by the trunk and the back, clashed nicely with bright pink flamingo lamps and wooden bears atop the bookshelf. Brad didn't care as long as she was happy.

She was also too impatient to wait for me to introduce her. "You must be Max." Sunny held out her hand, sizing him up before giving him a smile. "I'm Sunday."

"Excuse me?" Max looked at me for confirmation that he had heard correctly as he shook her hand.

"My name is Sunday, but everyone calls me Sunny."

"It was the day we were born," I explained. "Our parents are a bit odd, but I am forever thankful she came out first."

Max chuckled. "Why did they name you Chase?"

"Because he followed me out. And he's been chasing after me ever since," Sunny said with a wink.

"Not true."

"You followed me to Missouri."

I ignored that comment. We didn't talk about why I moved away from San Diego. "And this is her husband, Brad. But we call him St. Brad for putting up with my sister."

"Hush," she told me. "Your boyfriend's going to think we don't get along. When in fact, we are very close. Very close." She narrowed her eyes at Max. Was she trying to intimidate him? And did she really have to use the word 'boyfriend'?

My nieces ran in, distracting everyone, thankfully. "These are our daughters, Della and Cassie," Brad said.

The girls hugged me tightly. They wore their shiniest dresses, and I was sure they wanted to impress Max. He bent down to talk to each of them and they giggled adorably. He wasn't lying. The girls were already enamored.

"Dinner's almost ready," Brad said, leading them into the dining room.

"I was worried for a sec that their names might be Tuesday and Wednesday," he whispered to me.

I smacked his arm, but I couldn't hold in my giggle. The girls weren't the only ones charmed by Max. He was so self-assured, even with the nerves. He seemed at home wherever he went.

As expected, my sister drove the conversation in whatever direction she wanted. She was naturally bubbly and very talkative. The complete opposite of me. Max was able to keep up without a problem. He answered her questions, which weren't always appropriate.

"What's on the horizon for you two?"

"Sunny," I began.

"What do you mean?"

"I mean what's next?"

"Wait," Max said. "Is this the what's-your-intentions-toward-my-brother speech? I've been really looking forward to that."

"It is." She narrowed her eyes at him. "What are your intentions?"

I huffed out my disapproval, but they both ignored me.

"I want to spend as much time with him as I can for as long as he'll let me."

"That's enough, Sunny," I said firmly. My heart warmed at his answer, but I didn't need my sister to protect me. "This is all new, and we don't need you pushing it."

She held up her hands, defensively, not looking the least bit sorry, and changed the subject. We talked about music, television, and movies—safe enough topics. Or so I thought.

"Have you guys seen that forensic files show on TV? It's all about murders and how people get caught or not."

"If it's not home improvement, a show about cooking, or Star Wars," I said, "I probably haven't seen it."

"You like watching comedies with me." Max kissed my cheek and the girls giggled.

"Those are stupid. But I do enjoy watching them with

you." I mostly loved to listen to him laugh. His face would light up and his eyes crinkled at the edges. The man oozed sex all the time. How was I supposed to resist him? Our gazes locked until my sister cleared her throat.

"As I was saying before you guys started making out, I saw this really good episode. It had these twins on it."

I narrowed my eyes in warning. I didn't know where she was going with this, but I didn't trust her. Not one bit.

"You know Chase and I are twins," she said to Max.

"I did know that."

"Well, in the episode there were these twins and one of them had a really bad break up. So one of them murdered the ex-boyfriend."

"Sunny," I said. "Is this really appropriate?" I nodded toward the girls, but they weren't paying attention to us. They were arguing over whose dress had the most sparkles.

"It's fine." Sunny waved her hand. "The point is, the twin who did it actually got off because of the forensic evidence. The twins' DNA was so close, they couldn't rule out either one of them. They had introduced reasonable doubt, so they had no choice but to let both of them go."

"Sunday." I glared at my sister. She needed to stop talking. Wasn't it time to leave yet?

"I thought Max would find that story interesting," she said with a smile. "You know, in case he ever decided to hurt you."

"Doesn't that only work if you're identical twins?" Max didn't miss a beat.

"You really want to take that chance?" They stared at each other, neither backing down.

"All right, that's enough," Chase said. "I can take care of myself, Sunny."

"I have no doubt of that. But I also remember what happened last time."

"We're done with this conversation or we're leaving."

"Touchy."

"So, Max," Brad cut in. "You guys work in the same place, right? That's handy."

Max jumped on the subject change. "It's nice to get to see him every day." He reached down and squeezed my leg in support. "But it's also a little complicated since inter-office romances are forbidden."

"Really?" Sunny glanced over at me, eyebrows raised.

"Mind your own business."

"We're their two best employees. I think as long as we don't throw it in their faces, we'll be fine."

I squeezed his hand, smiling up at him. Max leaned in and kissed me. I didn't even care that Sunny watched me like I was a teenager on my first date.

The conversation turned to football. Sunny loved the sport. I watched it sometimes, but I didn't have a favorite team. Max and Sunny discussed quarterback stats and who was the best in each division. I didn't follow the conversation much. In spite of my sister's attempts at interference, the evening went well. There was no storming out, so it went better than most of the dinners we had when I dated Cameron.

"You okay?" Max whispered, his voice concerned.

It reminded me that Max was nothing like Cameron. He actually cared how I was feeling. I smiled up at him. "Perfect."

The rest of the dinner went smoothly, but I had one problem. I had to pee. And there was no way I was leaving Max alone with my sister. I should have thought about this before drinking the third glass of iced tea. Finally, my bladder had had enough, and I couldn't wait.

"Excuse me," I said standing up. Max stood up with me. What a gentleman. "I'm just going to the bathroom." I kissed his cheek and glared at my sister to behave.

I hurried as fast as I could, not sure I even had anything to worry about. I mean, she had already threatened to murder him if he hurt me, could it get any worse?

I arrived back at the table, but Max and my sister were gone. Brad motioned to the kitchen with an apologetic look. I sighed as I headed toward the kitchen to ward off trouble. I realized as I entered the room that I was too late.

FIFTEEN

Max

CHASE SEEMED AFRAID TO LEAVE ME alone with his sister. He gave us both nervous glances. I'd seen him squirming, but I just thought he was nervous. I smiled at him, trying to reassure him. He sighed and kissed me before darting from the room. I was sure he had nothing to worry about. I was wrong.

He was barely out the door when she spoke up.

"Max, can you give me a hand in the kitchen?" She was gathering up the plates.

I should have trusted Chase. As I followed her in, I wondered how bad it would be.

We put the plates on the kitchen counter by the sink.

"Do you want me to help you load the dishwasher?"

"No," she said, turning to me. "We don't have time for that. He'll be right back."

"Okay." I backed up, looking around for an escape plan if I needed it.

"I know I gave you a hard time about my brother before, but all joking aside..."

"That was you joking?"

"Mostly."

I wondered how long Chase would be in the bathroom. I also knew if he'd been in there with us, he would have been working on the dishes until they were done and the kitchen was spotless.

"Chase is a serious guy," she said. "If that's not what you want, if serious is not what you're looking for, get out now. I've picked up the pieces before, Max. I don't want to do it again."

"Don't you trust that Chase knows what he wants?"

"It's not Chase I'm worried about. It's you."

"Okay."

"You just don't seem like the white picket fence kind of guy. Am I wrong?"

I couldn't lie to her. "I've never been before."

"And you think Chase is the one?"

"I'd like to find out," I said. "Do I seem like I'm going to bolt?"

"Look, I'm gonna be honest with you. I can tell you care about him. A lot. I see it in the way you look at him. But I also see that fear in your eyes. You're afraid of where this can go."

I narrow my eyes at her. "Are you a witch?"

"I'm not answering that." She sighed. "I don't need your answer. It's none of my business."

"Really."

"Mostly none of my business. But again, I'm the one having to pick up the pieces when or if you leave."

"I'm not planning on going anywhere."

"I'm not sure I'm willing to take that chance."

"It's not up to you, Sunny. Your brother is stronger than you think. He's the fiercest person I know."

"I agree. But I'm worried he's already in too deep. If you are serious—welcome to the family. If not—get the hell out. That's all I wanted to say."

"What's going on in here?" Chase stood at the door, glaring at his sister.

"Nothing," Sunny said innocently. "Max is just helping me clean up."

Sunny pulled Chase aside as we were leaving. I didn't have to hear it to know she was warning him to be careful. Her words came back to me. She was right. Chase wanted to settle down. I didn't want to lose him, but could I give him what he needed? I'd never been one for commitment. Maybe that's because I hadn't met the right guy. Or maybe I'd bail one day and break Chase's heart. I couldn't imagine it now, but I'd never been with the same guy for over a week. Hell, it usually didn't last the weekend. Could I give Chase the rest of my life? Our relationship wasn't to that level. At all. But that's where it was heading for Chase; he didn't do casual. Sunny was right. If I wasn't in it for the long haul, I should get out now. But the thought of being without Chase caused my chest to tighten in panic.

Sunny trailed behind Chase as they joined us at the door. Chase rolled his eyes, and I bit back a laugh.

"It was nice meeting you, Max," Sunny said. She ignored my hand and hugged me. "Remember what I said," she whispered.

On our way back to the apartment, Chase apologized over and over. "I'm sorry. I should've warned you about my sister."

"I like that she's so protective of you." I squeezed his leg. I'd wanted to touch him all night, and I no longer had to restrain myself. "Wait until you meet my family. I have five siblings, although none of them are as intense as your sister."

"No one is. It's the twin thing. I was probably just as bad when she first met Brad."

Chase smiled at me as he maneuvered the car through traffic. He'd seemed nervous on the trip there, but now he didn't hesitate as he passed a slow-going semi on the highway. His confidence turned me on. Mostly because it meant he was comfortable with me enough not to stress over his driving. It also reminded me of Chase taking charge during sex. I squeezed his leg again before inching my hand up a little. Just enough to get my point across but not enough to get us into an accident.

"Max?" He took a few quick breaths. "What are you doing?"

"Foreplay?"

"While I'm driving?"

"You've got this, babe," I said, my thumb rubbing the side of his leg. "And we're almost there."

Chase's hand covered mine, and for a moment, I thought he was going to move it. Instead, he slotted his fingers between mine and moved our hands slightly closer to his straining erection. He bit his lip, his left hand clenching the steering wheel. I used my other hand to tuck his hair behind his ear and then I kissed his jaw.

"Are we there yet?" I asked in a low voice. I wanted to be home in bed with Chase pounding into me.

"Two blocks." His voice was slightly higher like he couldn't catch his breath.

We parked in the parking garage. Chase stared straight ahead, not moving. His hand relaxed on mine, giving me permission to do more. I slid my hand up his inner thigh slowly, until he was aching for more.

"Max," he said, spreading his legs. "Touch me."

I almost came right then. The guy was so sexy with his head back, eyes half closed, and the inviting flush on his skin. I traced the bulge in his pants with my thumb, slow at first and then faster. His breathing faltered as he pushed back against my hand. I covered his erection with my hand and squeezed. Chase let out a moan.

"Should we take this inside?" I whispered in his ear before biting down on the lobe.

"I... What?" His eyes closed tightly. "Please?" One hand still gripped the steering wheel. I loved that he was open, just giving himself to me.

"I'll take that as a no." I kissed his neck, licking and sucking as I trailed down his neck to his shoulder. Chase whimpered as I changed hands. Leaning closer, I used my right hand to flip open the button on his skinny jeans and slowly unzip them. My left hand ran through the hair on the top of his head. God, I loved his hair.

But I also loved his cock. I slipped my hand under his underwear and pulled his erection out. I couldn't wait any longer to touch him. Chase jerked up in my hand. Precum beaded on the tip of his cock and I wanted to lick it. The car was cramped, and I could tell Chase was already close, so I settled for swiping the tip with my thumb. He whined again, and I shushed him with a filthy kiss. My tongue stroked his as I jerked him off.

I pulled away to take a breath, resting my head on his shoulder. "You're so gorgeous, babe," I said, stroking him faster. He looked vulnerable as he arched his back, his body spread out in front of me, trembling under my touch.

"Napkins. Console." He could barely string words together, and yet he worried about getting his pants, or maybe just his car, messy. It was adorable.

I grabbed the napkins out of the console with my free hand. He seemed to let go then, moaning out my name as he came. I kissed him again, wiping the sweaty strands of his long hair off his face.

He smiled at me. "Thank you."

I helped clean him up and threw the napkins in a trash bag he had in his car. Everything about him was neat and clean except when I dirtied him up. It was one of my favorite things to do.

"Ready to continue this upstairs? In bed?" I asked.

"Lead the way."

It took way longer than I wanted to continue what we'd started in the car. We had to take Toby out and Chase insisted we wash the dishes I'd left from breakfast. But eventually we made it to bed and I was able to show Chase just how much I wanted him.

I couldn't tell if meeting Chase's family was a success or not. It could go either way. I liked them but they were different from what I expected. Especially, Sunny. Since they were twins, I expected them to be more alike. They were quite different. Sunny was outgoing and she said what she thought. Although Chase did to a point, he was very careful about everything he said and whom he said it to. He didn't talk unless it was necessary. He was more of an introvert, whereas Sunny seemed more of an extrovert.

Chase had a seriousness about him that I loved, but he still liked to laugh. He didn't take our relationship lightly. This wasn't just a fling to him. Normally that would have me running for the hills. There was something about having that ongoing relationship, the intimacy I'd never experienced before. Chase made all the difference. I really didn't want to screw this up. For one thing, Sunny would have me for breakfast if I did. And for another, I couldn't imagine not having Chase in my life.

Over the next week, we slowed things down at work. Our sups were getting suspicious. Chase had stopped at my desk to say good morning. He'd stayed home the night before. His excuse was because he wanted to clean. I believed him. The man loved having everything spotless. It was calming for him. I'd slept late, restless without him, and missed him at the elevator. Chase was leaning over my desk, laughing at something I'd said when Sean walked by. He shook his head, closing his eyes briefly, like he wanted to pretend it wasn't happening. Then signs had started appearing on the doors of the copy room, the storage room, and the breakroom. They all said the same thing:

THIS DOOR IS TO BE OPEN AT ALL TIMES

Chase had been worried, but I assured him that if management had any proof, we would have already been called in to their offices.

It was difficult keeping my hands to myself, but it helped knowing I got to have him with me every night. Toby also seemed hooked on Chase. He barely barked at him now. Instead, he danced around his legs, tail wagging. We'd done domesticated things together like taking Toby to the park and getting him new jackets to wear. Chase even found a thunder shirt, which was weighted to help ease anxiety in dogs. I waited to feel the usual panic that settled in when I thought of spending the rest of my life like this. It didn't happen. At least not yet.

We went out to dinner a few times. Chase was insistent we still do the things I loved to do. I didn't really care as long as he was with me, but he seemed to have something to prove to himself. We loved going to the Italian restaurant. My neighbor Janice offered to stay with Toby to help ease any anxiety. I hadn't ever thought of doing that before, but it worked like a charm. Not that we stayed gone for too long.

It was the one-month anniversary of our first official date, and we sat at a small table at Santinos. The monthly performance metrics had been released at work, and Chase once again topped the list. It didn't bother me as much anymore, and I loved seeing him happy. He was telling me about a customer who couldn't figure out "The Google," gesturing wildly with his hands.

"Max?"

I glanced over at the guy who'd stopped at our table. He had shoulder-length, brown, wavy hair and dark eyes. I recognized him instantly, but I still couldn't remember his name.

"Hi..." I hesitated, hoping his name would pop in my head. Lee? Levi? Neither seemed correct.

"Nathan," he said, his smile slipping as he glanced over at Chase. "It's only been a month or so. You've already forgotten me?"

What could I say to that? *I forgot you as soon as you left my bed* was the truth but not the right thing to say. Especially with Chase watching me with raised eyebrows. Shit. I really didn't need him to be reminded of my old playboy ways.

"It's nice to see you again, Nathan." I kept my voice neutral. I just needed him gone as soon as possible. We'd been having a good time before he showed up. "This is Chase."

Nathan regarded him coolly. "Is this the new flavor of the month? Excuse me, I mean day."

Chase's cheeks flushed. I wasn't sure if it was embarrassment or anger. Maybe both.

I glared at the twins. There was no reason for him to be this catty. I'd never made any promises to him.

"This is my boyfriend," I said through gritted teeth. "And I think it's time you moved along."

"Boyfriend," he scoffed. "You?"

I stood up, towering over him. I usually didn't ever try to intimidate anyone, but this guy was pushing my buttons. "Leave."

Nathan rolled his eyes before turning to Chase. "Good luck," he said. "Seriously. You're going to need it."

Once he left, I turned to Chase. "I'm sorry, babe."

"Was it really only a month ago?"

"It was more than a month," I said. He raised his eyebrows again, and I sighed. "But not much longer than that. I slept around. I can't deny it. But there's been no one else but you since we first went out.

He nodded, but I could see the doubt in his eyes.

"You're the only one I want, Chase."

"At least you remember my name." Chase winked at me.

After that night, I caught Chase staring at me with questions whenever we were around a guy I knew. Was he wondering who I slept with? Wouldn't I be doing the same? I knew Chase hadn't been in a serious relationship since his breakup, but maybe he'd hooked up. The thought made me sick. I didn't want anyone else touching Chase. Was this how he felt. I didn't want him to feel like he wasn't good enough. I tried to reassure him in every way, every interaction that we had that he was special.

We snuggled on the couch with Toby between us when I asked the question I'd had for a while. "Why did you leave San Diego?" Thankfully, his sister had mentioned where they were from or he might wonder how I knew.

He hesitated, adjusting Toby on his lap. "My parents aren't really supportive," he said. "Sunny had moved here. It's where Brad is from."

I slid my hand through his hair, trying to reassure him. I could tell it was difficult to talk about.

"I thought I could do it on my own." He shrugged. "But I was lonely, and I'm not so good at making friends. Sunny talked me in to moving here."

"And by talked you mean bullied."

"Yes," he said with a laugh.

"They didn't approve of you being gay?"

He looked up at me. Tears were in his eyes, and I kissed his cheek. "It wasn't that. They didn't care at all that I was gay."

That surprised me. "I don't understand."

"It was my anxiety. They thought I should be able to just get over it."

I hugged him tightly. I couldn't imagine how hard that was for him. No one to support him and his anxiety keeping him from reaching out to anyone.

I kissed his temple. "You have lots of support now." Toby licked his arm, putting in his two cents' worth.

I'd resisted having Chase meet my family. Not because I was ashamed of him in any way. It had more to do with my siblings embarrassing me. I also wanted to keep Chase to myself for a while. I'd never brought anyone home before. It was a big deal. I realized he thought it had more to do with how serious I was about him. He'd brought it up several times. Finally, I relented. There were so many people in my family it was sometimes overwhelming. How would Chase react when he didn't even like crowds? I negotiated with my mom to keep it to a few family members to ease Chase into it. She'd been ecstatic that I finally found someone, so was ready to agree to anything.

My mom planned a small lunch of pulled pork and the fixings that went with it on Sunday afternoon. My family loved their barbecue.

"Are you sure you want to meet my family?" I asked for the hundredth time.

"Don't you think they'll like me?"

I hugged him. I hated when he looked unsure, like he wasn't good enough. "I'm just gonna be honest with you. I've never brought anyone home before. They are going to be like vultures."

"Sounds like fun."

I shook my head. Might as well get it over with. "All my

siblings won't be there. Just my mom and dad and a few others. I'm not sure exactly who's showing up, to tell you the truth."

"But your parents know you're gay, right?"

"They will now." I laughed at Chase's panicked look. "I'm kidding. They know I'm gay."

Chase smacked me, causing Toby to bark. At me. Traitor. "Get him Tobias," Chase said with a laugh.

I wrestled Chase onto the couch, tickling him. Toby jumped on the couch, trying to rescue him. My touches became more intimate as I accidentally grazed his cock.

"Stop it, Maxwell." He turned us over, so he was sitting on my lower body. He grabbed both my hands and pinned them over my head. I could have easily gotten out of his hold, but why would I have wanted to? "We need to get ready to go."

"If this is your way of convincing me to be good, I think my cock is getting mixed signals." I squirmed against him, pushed my growing erection into his ass.

"Maybe we have a few minutes to spare," he said, sounding breathless. "But let's take it to your room so Toby doesn't think you're trying to hurt me."

"He's my dog," I grumbled.

An hour later, we were ready to go. My heart pounded in my chest. Was I really taking a boy home to meet Mom and Dad? Yes. Yes, I was. And although I was thrilled I had found someone to take home to the parents, I was also terrified. I could so easily fuck this up.

What was I worried about? Even if my family didn't like Chase, which wasn't possible, it didn't matter. They would just have to deal with it because I wasn't giving him up.

Chase smiled at me as he took my hand. "It'll be fine," he said.

"Famous last words."

"I think it's cute, Max. I don't think I've ever seen you this nervous."

We took my car, but Chase drove. My stomach churned the closer we got to my parents' home. Chase squeezed my hand.

"It'll be fine," he said again. And I almost believed him.

Yet there was something at the back of my mind that wouldn't let me relax. Was it because I didn't feel I really deserved Chase? It couldn't be about my past. Chase knew about that and had accepted me. I didn't figure it out until after we got in the house, and I introduced him to my mom.

"Hello, Mrs. Sloan," Chase said. "It's so nice to meet you."

She practically beamed at him. "Call me Diane, hon." She hugged him like he was a long-lost son. "It's so nice to meet you. Max has never brought anyone home before."

"Mom." I shook my head at her, but she ignored my warning and hugged me. After she moved to the side, ushering us farther into the house, Carole and her husband came in with smiles on their faces. That's when my world fell apart.

How could I forget? More importantly, how could I avert the impending disaster?

"Mac," my sister said, giving me a hug. Chase glanced over at me, his eyebrows drawn as if he was trying to figure something out. *Fuck.* I'd forgotten about my nickname. The one I'd also given to Chase over the phone as a completely different person. I was such an idiot.

"This is Chase," I said quickly, trying to keep Chase from thinking too much about it. "Chase this is my sister Carole and her husband." I'd left off his name intentionally, but it didn't matter. There was no way to stop this train wreck. But could I minimize the damage?

Carole hugged him. My brother-in-law held out his hand. "Howard," he said, giving me a strange look. "And this is our daughter, Penny." Their only child was twelve and precocious. And she was one of my favorites.

Mom returned to the kitchen to check on the food. We made it to the living room, where my dad and my youngest sister were. As I made introductions, I tried to figure out what to do next. It was all going to come out. Howard was a common name. Hernandez was not. But there was always a chance Chase wouldn't remember the call. Right? The same call in which I had flirted with Chase and asked him out. I wanted to slam my head against the wall. The pain would be a nice diversion.

Everyone in the room called me Mac. Chase asked about the nickname, and I told him the story of how I'd gotten it. He smiled but it didn't seem sincere. Did he remember the name from the call, or was he just upset I hadn't told him about it in the first place? Only my family called me that, so I hadn't thought to mention it to him. I wished I had remembered. Then I could have prepared him for this exact moment. No time like the present.

"Chase?" I cleared my throat, trying to sound less like a dying man. "Could I talk to you for a moment?" If I could somehow control the information, explain it to him on my terms, it might not be too bad. I took a deep breath, trying to relax my racing heart.

"Are you okay?"

"Yes," I said. "I just wanted to tell you something." I don't know why I didn't foresee this happening. I had to tell him no matter what. I didn't want this secret between us. I tried to pull him toward the hallway leading away from the living room and the crowd, when my mom returned.

"Dinner's ready."

"Come on," Chase said. "We can talk later."

I nodded, giving up for now. Maybe it would be fine.

Lunch was lively with chatter and laughter. Chase

answered questions with a smile on his face about his family and growing up in San Diego. So much attention was on him, and affection rushed through me. He was doing this for me.

I leaned over and gave him a quick kiss, ignoring the sighs from Greta and Penny.

"What was that for?"

"I know this is hard for you," I whispered. "Thank you so much for coming."

"Of course." Chase squeezed my hand under the table.

"Tell us how you two met."

I wanted to throttle my sister, but I should have expected the question. If not from a sibling, from my mom. They glanced at each other every once in a while, identical conspiring looks on their faces. They probably had a list of questions.

"Max mistook me for a woman," Chase said.

"Really?" Greta asked. Everyone laughed.

"No, not really. I knew he was a guy."

"That's his story," Chase said with a wink. "It's my long hair. That mistake happens more than you think."

"What happened?" Greta loved romance books and movies. She was eating this up.

Chase smiled. "Max called me beautiful."

"I bet that went over well," Carole said.

"Exactly how you'd think."

"I'd love for someone to call me beautiful." Penelope had a dreamy look on her face.

"You're only twelve," Howard reminded her.

"Yes," Chase said, smiling at her. "But I knew right away, Max was a player."

"*Was* being the important word there." I loved the smile on his face. I wished I could keep it there forever. "Then he turned and looked at me like he wanted to slit my throat. Or stomp me with his little black boots."

"You remember the shoes I wore that day?"

"I remember everything."

"Oh, really?"

"You had on slim-fitting black pants and a purple button-down shirt with tiny birds on them. And never once did I think you were a woman."

"But he let me think that. We didn't like each other very much, at first."

"What changed?" Penny leaned into her arms on the table.

"Max is very persistent." Everyone nodded in agreement, and Chase laughed. "Finally, he just wore me down."

Greta and Penny smiled like it was the greatest story they'd ever heard.

The conversation moved around then. My dad talked about his recent trips to the doctor. They were monitoring his blood pressure. Carole engaged the girls in talking about a new movie they both wanted to see. I was happy to stay on the sidelines, sneaking glances at Chase and wanting to lick the barbecue sauce off his chin.

"This girl has been driving me crazy," Penny said. "I don't know what her problem is, but I finally had enough and stopped her after gym class on Friday."

"You confronted her?" Chase asked. "I'm impressed. I could never have done that at your age."

"It's the Hernandez way," Howard said.

The noise continued around them, but Chase sat perfectly still. *Shit.*

"What did you say?" he asked.

"The Hernandez way. We come from a long line of fighters. Tact is not our strong suit."

"Your name is Howard Hernandez?"

"Yes."

"From Hudson Lane."

"Yes." He drew the word out in question.

"Chase," I said. He was putting two and two together, and I wanted to do something. Anything. He held up his hand for me to stop, not even glancing my way.

"Do you have problems with your Internet, Howard?"

Now it was Howard's turn to look confused. "No. Not really."

"So, you haven't called the call center?"

"No." He thought for a second. "Oh, wait," he said. "I remember now."

Chase glanced at Howard and turned to look at Carole. I could tell what he was thinking. This guy had hit on him. Had asked him out and yet he was married.

"Chase," I said again. But this time I was interrupted by my brother-in-law.

"Max called, using my account." No one said a word or moved. Everyone was quiet.

Chase's face was slashed red, and I wanted to reach out to him. "I don't understand," he said.

Howard laughed, not catching on to the serious mood. "Me either. Max was pulling a prank or something on some guy."

"A prank." Chase sounded broken.

"Not a prank," I said, trying to touch him, but he pulled away.

"Right," Howard agreed. "It was some stuck-up guy Max didn't like. Ice Princess. I think that's what they called him. He wanted to take him down a peg."

"Howard." Carole grabbed his arm. "Shut up."

Chase stood up suddenly, his chair scraping on the dining room tile. "I'm sorry," he said. "I have to go."

I tried to rush after him, but my family had other ideas. "What's going on, Max?" my mom asked.

"It's him." Carole looked at me with pity in her eyes. "Chase is the guy you pranked."

"Maxwell." My mom opened her mouth to tell me off, but I didn't have time for this.

I raced out the front door. I had to catch him. I couldn't lose him.

Chase stood on the curb of my mom's suburban home, his arms wrapped protectively around him. He wiped at his eyes.

"Chase. Let me explain."

He shook his head. "I can't talk to you right now."

"I know you're upset. Let me drive you home." I moved closer, trying not to crowd him. I just wanted to hug him. To explain. But what could I say really?

"I called an Uber."

"You hate being alone with strangers. Especially in a confined space."

He turned to me; his eyes sparked with rage. "And yet it's preferable to being alone with you right now."

I wanted to erase the pain in his eyes. It hurt knowing I put it there.

The Uber driver arrived and without a backward glance, Chase got in the back seat and the car sped away. I wanted to rush after them, but the only thing I could do was let him go. When he calmed down, I could talk to him. It took everything I had to go back inside the house.

"I'm sorry, man," Howard said. "I didn't realize that was the guy. Seriously, you should have just told me."

"It's not your fault. It's mine. All of this is my fault." I glanced around at all the worried faces of my family.

"Is Chase coming back?" Carole asked.

"No. He took an Uber home." I kissed my mom's cheek and hugged my dad goodbye. "Thanks for everything, guys. Sorry for the drama," I said, turning to leave.

"Max?"

I didn't turn around. I couldn't bear the pity in their eyes.

"Just give him some time."

I snuggled on the couch with Toby. If he knew what I'd done, he would be mad at me, too. Good thing dogs loved unconditionally, even when you did asshole things. The TV was on in the background, but I wasn't listening to it. I replayed the scene over and over in my mind, wondering how Chase was doing. He must feel horrible right now.

I had always been afraid of commitment. Afraid of getting hurt. It never really made sense. My parents had been happily together for more than thirty years. I'd seen my friends go through relationship after relationship, but I didn't think that was it. I hated failing at anything, and I didn't like not being the one in control. When you loved someone as much as my parents loved each other, you definitely gave up control.

It hit me then. I loved Chase. This was exactly what I'd been afraid of, and yet I wouldn't trade any moment I'd had with him to erase the pain. The only thing I could think about was how to get him back.

SIXTEEN

Chase

THE RIDE HOME WAS AWFUL BUT NOT for the reason I expected. I hated riding in an Uber, with a total stranger, by myself. I usually either stressed about making small talk or worried the guy was an ax murderer. Those things never crossed my mind. I was too busy nursing my broken heart. It had all been a game to him. A prank. It certainly wasn't the first prank Max had played on me.

It never crossed my mind that it wasn't real. That wasn't true. I'd wondered if it was real. It had been too good to be true. The worry that Max was just playing me had been my greatest fear. Somehow, he worked his way past my defenses, and I had believed him.

No wonder Max hadn't wanted to have sex with me. It was all a game. And I threw myself at him. Was he even attracted to me?

But a part of me still had a hard time believing it. There was no way Max could have faked everything. Sure, he could have imagined someone else when we'd had sex, but those little moments when I'd catch Max watching me. The soft touches. The sweet words.

It didn't matter. Even if part of it had been real, which I wasn't ready to believe, Max had lied to me. He'd pretended to be someone else for a prank. His goal? Wasn't it obvious? He wanted to be number one again. And he got everything he wanted. He distracted me. I even flirted with a customer. All he had to do was send my boss an anonymous tip, and I would be sacked.

The whole office was probably in on it. Were they all laughing at me behind my back? Dylan and Sadie? Everyone?

While my heart was breaking in two, part of me rejected the notion. Why would Max bring me to meet his family when it could expose him? Why did he go to meet my family?

Max wasn't honest with me, and he had plenty of chances. Even if at some point his feelings changed, I couldn't trust him. And I wasn't going through that again. Never knowing what was real and what was not.

I made it home in one piece. I usually cleaned to help me focus, but I was too exhausted for even that. I curled up in my bed in my favorite pajamas. I turned my phone off. If Max called, I didn't want to talk to him. I might never be ready to talk to him. Or he might not call. That might just be worse. Whatever happened, I could deal with it tomorrow. I gave myself permission to cry myself to sleep. Just this once. After that, I would toughen my heart. Pull myself together. If I had to act like Max didn't exist, I could do it. I've done it before.

The next day I felt like I'd been hit with a sledgehammer. Everything hurt, but mostly my heart. It would take more than one night to get over Max. It didn't help that I had a dozen missed calls and texts from him. I didn't even read them. What was the point? I couldn't believe anything he said. I also had a missed call from my sister. I wasn't ready to talk to her either. I put the pillow back over my head. What was the point of even getting out of bed?

I also had a message from Amica. It was short, just asking

how I was doing and offering to talk. Max must have called her and told her what had happened. Heat burned through my cheeks. I was so humiliated. I didn't want to go to work. Everyone probably already knew.

I needed to get my act together. I'd survived before. Cameron wanted me to be something I wasn't. Now here was Max pretending to be something he wasn't. I was done with men. I refused to let another one stomp all over my heart. My inner circle was small for a reason. People sucked. And I was tired of being hurt.

In the end, I went in to work. No way would I give Max that satisfaction. I retreated back into my old self, before Max. That was the way it had to be. I'd let Max into my circle, my bubble, my heart and look at what happened. Max crushed it. Would I ever feel safe enough to let someone else in?

Most people didn't even notice the change. They went about their day as if the world hadn't ended. As if my world hadn't ended. But there were a few who noticed. As I was getting my morning coffee, Amica cornered me in the lounge.

"Hey, Chase. Are you okay?"

"I'm fine," I said, not looking her in the eyes. I couldn't stand to see the pity there. I didn't need to be reminded of the poor decisions I'd made.

"Max called me."

I sighed. "I'm not surprised."

"Do you want to talk about it? This has to be hard for you."

"No," I said, putting sugar in my coffee and stirring. I tried not to look at my Yoda cup. It reminded me of Max. "I don't want to talk about it. It's over. The end."

"Is it?" Amica touched my hand, violating my don't-touch-me rule, but I let it slide. She was just trying to help.

I turned toward her, finally meeting her eyes. There was

sadness there but also a spark of anger. At Max? She'd always been protective of me.

"Is it, Chase?" she asked again. "Is it over?"

"I think so." I tried to keep the tears at bay. I was not going to cry over Maxwell Sloan. "How can I trust him? Everything he said and did was suspect. Was I supposed to believe he became so enamored, he forgot about his prank? His quest to be number one?"

"Max is a jackass," she said. "But I think you should give him a chance to explain, Chase."

"Why? Give me one good reason."

"Because I've never seen you that happy before."

The tears threatened again, and I blinked them away. "It wasn't real," I said. "None of it was real."

"I don't think that's true."

I pulled my hand away. "Amica," I said, not unkindly, "I have to get through today without crying. You could help with that by not talking to me about Max."

The walk back to my cubicle took forever. Was everyone watching me? But when I chanced a look at them, no one was paying attention. While I was glad, so glad, that everyone at work wasn't focused on my life, my world had shifted. I was devastated and no one noticed. God, I was a mess. I shook off the melancholy that threatened to overwhelm me. I had a job to do. People to help. I would do it and damn Max for making me think otherwise.

Work was a relief. I was good at fixing people's problems. I helped them get what they needed and made their life better in the process. It was the distraction I needed, and it helped me feel better about myself. I wasn't a complete failure. I wasn't a complete idiot. Yes, I fell for Max and all his promises, all his lies, just like I did with Cameron, but I also learned something. People weren't to be trusted after all. I would just have to be more careful.

I stayed in my cubicle for lunch. We weren't really supposed to do that, but Gina did it all the time and no one said anything to her. I didn't really eat anyway. I wasn't hungry, so I just had a few bites of a sandwich I'd brought from home. I couldn't face anyone, most of all Max. Part of it was because I hated him. I hated how he made me doubt myself. And a part of me worried that Max would tell me what I wanted to hear and fool me all over again. I couldn't go through it again. I had been in too deep already, letting myself believe there was a future for us.

It was already so hard. We'd only been apart one day, and I already missed him. Missed the way he smelled. The way he liked to run his fingers through my hair. I'd felt so lucky to be with Max. Finished with my sandwich, I threw my trash away. I had to throw those thoughts of Max away, too. My heart couldn't take any more. If I let Max back in, it could destroy me.

I was making copies for the next day's presentation, when I realized my mistake. Max must have been watching me because he was suddenly right there behind me. My body reacted before my brain caught up. It was the way he smelled. The way he sounded when he walked.

"Chase? Please talk to me."

"I'm busy," I said, finally turning to face him. "I have a presentation to prepare for."

"We're doing that presentation together," Max reminded me.

I kept my cool. Not giving an inch. "Is it about the presentation?"

"We should probably talk about it..."

"Fine. Email me."

"Chase, please." He touched my hand.

I pulled back, afraid of the sparks I always felt when Max touched me. Today was no different. Didn't my body get the memo that Max was bad news? "Don't."

"I want to explain."

I didn't want to hear it, but he would never leave it alone. "Fine."

Max's eyes went wide and for the first time since I'd known him, he didn't say anything.

"Well?"

"I...I didn't expect you to agree."

"I shouldn't have." I gathered my papers and turned to leave. Max's hand brushed mine before I yanked it back.

"It wasn't a prank," he said.

"Then what was it? You were so enamored that you had to talk to me?"

"Not exactly."

That hurt more than I expected.

"I couldn't figure you out. Customers loved you but were bitchy to everyone else."

"That's what you're going with?" I said. I willed back the tears and reached for the anger instead. "You have a chance and that's what you tell me?"

"I want to be honest with you."

"It's a little late for that." I crossed my arms, holding tightly to my copies.

"I wanted to understand you. You were always at the top in customer service."

"You wanted to bring me down a peg or two?" This time I couldn't stop my eyes from welling up. Great.

"No. Honestly. I told Howard that because I was too embarrassed to admit you were better than me. I wanted to know how you did it. I didn't mean to hurt you."

"Well," I said. "Thanks for being honest." I reached the

door when Max was once again behind me. "You were a challenge at first. But that changed when I talked to you."

I stopped but I didn't turn around. I cursed myself for wanting to hear the rest. "And?"

"I couldn't stop thinking about you. I still can't. I need you, Chase."

"You only need yourself, Max," I said, turning on him. "You are honestly the most self-centered person I've ever met."

"That's rich coming from you." Max didn't wait for me to leave. He stormed past me. Max was angry? At me? That bothered me way more than it should.

SEVENTEEN

Max

WELL, THAT WENT WELL.

I thought talking to Chase, being close to him, having the chance to explain my actions would make everything better. But in some ways, it made it worse.

I just wanted to be honest with him. I wanted to tell him the truth. And the truth was I acted like an ass, thinking only of myself. But in the end, I lost my temper. I was self-centered, I could admit that, but hearing it from Chase pissed me off. Not that Chase didn't think of other people, because he did. But Chase made his world small and it absolutely revolved around him. Understandably, so. Point was, I could have handled that better. And now I probably wouldn't get another chance.

I was lost without Chase. I hadn't realized how much I'd fallen until I no longer had him in my life. Everything reminded me of Chase. Absolutely everything. Hell, I couldn't make copies without wanting to cry. I sat in the breakroom for lunch and breaks, mostly hoping to get a chance to see Chase. My friends sat with me, mostly ignoring my moods, as the conversations swirled around me. No one seemed to mind that I didn't participate.

Dylan smacked me on the arm. "Dude, you have to snap out of it."

"You're right," I said, then continued moping. It wasn't that I didn't want to snap out of it. I just wanted to nurse my hurt feelings a little longer. Not that I blamed Chase for being mad. What I did was horrible and unfeeling. But the fact that Chase could throw away what we had so easily made my chest hurt. Did he really believe that everything was a lie when I was more truthful in every word, in every touch I shared with Chase, than I had been my whole life?

In the past I wore a mask. I charmed people, saying what they wanted to hear. I was good at reading people. Except for Chase. But the thing was with Chase, I didn't have to be that way. I let my guard down, and I was able to be myself, something people rarely saw. I'd let a few in. Dylan and Sadie, my family, and most recently Amica. But never had I let anyone in that I'd slept with. Except for Chase. I'd given so much of myself to him, and he threw it away. He couldn't see past the mistakes I'd made.

I loved Chase. I wasn't sure I wanted to go on without him. Not that I'd ever do anything drastic; I just wasn't used to the pain. It was like flexing a new muscle. I'd never really felt it before. It was like I'd lost a part of myself. How do people do this all the time? I didn't ever want to feel like this again. And yet, without Chase, this would be my life. Even if Chase forgave me, there was always the possibility of this happening again. I just wanted to lock myself in my room and never come out. But that wasn't me. I liked being around people. I craved the excitement. The attention. The interesting conversations. I loved crowds. I fed off the energy. But I didn't feel like hanging out with anyone who wasn't Chase.

Did Chase have anyone to talk to? Or would he just sit

alone in his room. Was he able to shut off his emotions? Maybe I never meant that much to him. It was something he tried and didn't work. But Chase had been devastated when he broke up with Cameron, and it had been his decision. It took him two years before he could trust anyone again. My heart hurt all over again at the thought. I did this to him. I was the one to blame. I had no right to yell at Chase. If there was anything I could do to fix it, I would. But talking to Chase right now would get me nowhere. He needed space.

One thing I knew for sure. I wasn't giving up on him.

The next day I didn't feel much better. My head pounded mostly because I couldn't sleep and when I did, I had dreams of Chase telling me to go away, and that he never wanted to see me again. My heart raced and my head pounded. I took a deep breath. It was only a dream and all things were possible again.

I didn't want to do anything to upset the delicate balance we had. Chase didn't hate me. At least I didn't think so. I didn't want to push him over that edge. Somehow, I had to make this right. The presentation was this afternoon. This might be my chance.

"Are you ready?" Dylan asked as we sat in the breakroom for lunch. Amica joined them. Mostly because Chase had decided never to eat lunch again. At least, not in the breakroom.

"I think we're ready." Amica smiled, but I could tell it was halfhearted. She didn't feel very cheerful. None of them did.

"What about Chase?" I asked. "Is he ready?"

She shrugged. "I'm sure his part is done, because this is Chase. But is he ready to do a presentation, especially one that you're involved in? I'm not sure about that."

"Harsh." Dylan shook his head.

"I'm calling it, like I see it."

"I'm sure you're right," I said. "I know Chase will be

prepared. And my being there will make everything harder for him."

"You could go home sick." We both stared at Dylan. "What?" he said. "I'm just saying, you could."

"This is going to sound terrible." I drummed my fingers on the table, trying to figure out how to say it. "This will be uncomfortable for Chase, but I'm not sure I care."

Amica and Dylan exchange looks. "Right," Dylan said. "You don't care."

"This is one of the only chances I have of getting close to him again. To show him how important he is to me. I'm not throwing it away because it makes him uncomfortable."

"I'd love to be in that room," Dylan said. "Heck and heck yeah."

"That's really not a thing people say."

"It's totally not," Amica agreed.

"I think it's catching on." Dylan shook his head. "You guys will all be in there, and I have to wait until later to hear about it. Amica, I'm depending on you to give the intel. Who knows what shape Max will be in. If it goes wrong, he's not going to want to talk about it."

"Thanks for the confidence builder."

"Do you have a plan?"

"I'm more of a doer than a planner, to be honest," I said.

"Yeah. Look how that turned out for you."

The presentation started off well enough. Chase and I were presenting the mentoring program, and Amica and Jon were presenting on how to keep it going and who should be included.

Chase and I went first. We split up the PowerPoint presentation with me going first and then Chase adding his part. I hoped we could prevent any awkward problems since it was divided up. Still, the way Chase avoided eye contact with me and shied away from me any time I got close was apparent. I didn't want our bosses to notice. But when Sean's eyes narrowed the second time Chase walked around me like I had an infectious disease, I knew it was too much to ask.

I finished my section and turned to Chase. "Was there anything I left out?"

"No," Chase said, his voice clipped. "You covered that adequately."

I motioned for Chase to join me, but he wouldn't move until I sat down. Way to be obvious.

"As you know, Mr. Sloan and I have been working on this to help tailor the mentor to the person. Some may want a hands-on approach as we discussed, and some may be nervous having someone follow them on a call. Unless there are specific concerns about a worker, we'd like to honor that. Each worker would have exactly what they need. Our goal would be to increase worker satisfaction and decrease turnover. Here are some ways we can support workers during the call and ways we support workers without getting on the call. This includes preparing them and then debriefing with them after they have their call." He pushed the button on the remote to change the slide. "Here is a list of questions we developed to ask the worker to help them define any issues they may have had and to strengthen those skills they already have."

He really was beautiful. I tried to follow along with the questions the others had but really all I could think about was Chase and his sweet lips and having him inside me. Those were dangerous thoughts, especially since Chase couldn't stand the sight of me. I was proud of how well he was doing, even with a broken heart. Unless Chase wasn't heartbroken. If I didn't mean anything to him. But I couldn't think that way.

Not when I could remember what it was like to hold Chase in my arms.

"Do you agree with that Max?" Sean asked, staring pointedly at me.

Crap. Should I go along with it or admit that I wasn't paying attention? Chase stared at me, his mouth set in a grim line as if daring me to contradict him.

"I think Chase is absolutely correct." I hoped I wasn't agreeing to something terrible, which was possible. Chase could have told them to fire me right now. He seemed to despise me enough for that.

"Interesting," Sean said. "Thank you, both. Now we will have Amica and Jon present.

After they were finished and the supervisors left, promising to get back with us, we started putting the equipment away. Chase slammed things around while he worked, and Amica gave me a questioning look. I shrugged.

"If you two have this under control, I think Jon and I will go back to discuss some ideas for implementation."

"We will?" Jon asked.

Chase wasn't paying attention to us as he wound the cords up.

Amica gave Jon a pointed look and then nodded her head toward Chase.

"Oh, right, yes. Absolutely. We have things to discuss. Important things."

Amica rolled her eyes as she pulled him out of the room.

"What's wrong?" I asked.

"As if you don't know."

"Chase, I don't know how many times I can apologize. I'm sorry. I never meant to hurt you."

Chase slammed his laptop into his backpack and turned toward me, his eyes furious. "You think that's what I'm mad about?" He took a deep breath and flexed at his fingers, staring back at me. "I mean, I'm still mad about that don't get me wrong, but the way you acted this afternoon." He shook his head. "Unbelievable."

"What did I do?" I thought back to the presentation and every single thing I said. I couldn't think of anything. What was he talking about?

"Really." Chase put his hands on his hips and glared at me. "So, you don't remember agreeing with me at the end of our presentation?"

"Yes," I said slowly, still trying to figure out what he was mad about. "What's wrong with agreeing with you?"

Chase shut his eyes as if he was trying to keep his cool. "I told them you had done a lot of the work and deserved most of the credit."

Crap. And I agreed with him. It made me look like a jerk who thought Chase didn't deserve any of the credit. "Why would you say anything like that? It's not even true."

"First of all," Chase said, "I was being polite and giving you credit. If you'd been listening and not scheming, then you would've known that."

"Let me get this straight. You said I did most of the work so that I could come back and say that you deserved the credit. That's some passive-aggressive bullshit right there."

"I wouldn't expect you to understand, Max. You've never given anybody any credit." Chase grabbed his bag to leave.

"That is absolutely not true." I reached for Chase's arm to stop him from leaving.

"Get your hands off me."

"No. Not until you listen to me." But I moved my hands away. I locked eyes with Chase. "You're right," I said. "I wasn't paying attention and I'm sorry."

"This was really important to me, Max. And all you had to do was do your job. Pay attention. And you couldn't even do that." He shook his head and started to move away.

"I was thinking about you. I struggle every single day, every single hour, every single minute. All I think about is you. I miss you so much."

Chase studied the floor, but I could see the tears in his eyes.

"Please give me a chance," I said softly, wanting to reach out to him, but not daring to.

Chase shook his head. "I can't. Not yet." He walked out, leaving me alone in the room.

It was the yet part, though, that gave me hope. Chase wasn't writing us off completely. Maybe, just maybe, there was a chance.

EIGHTEEN
Chase

I RUSHED INTO THE BATHROOM. It was the only place to get any privacy. I tried not to make any noise as the tears ran down my face. I didn't know what to do about Max. I was still so angry at him, so sure it was all just a ploy. When Max agreed that he'd done all the work on the project, I was livid. It was just like Max to take the credit, to be the showoff. But was Max really like that? It certainly made more sense that he wasn't paying attention. I wanted to believe what Max said, that he was thinking about me all the time. That he missed me.

But was it real? Or was Max just saying what he thought I wanted to hear? I'd seen Max do that over and over again with people. He was just so charming, so good with everyone, that it seemed fake. My heart wanted to believe that Max cared about me. That Max meant everything he said to me. And there were times when I just wanted to give in and let Max tell me what I wanted so desperately to hear.

But then I'd think back to Cameron. He'd always talk me out of being angry. He'd apologize later, saying sweet things. He'd say it was his own fault for not understanding what I was going through. He'd promise to try harder. And yet, he never really tried to understand. It was just words to say to manipulate me. I couldn't go through that again. I wouldn't.

I dried up my tears and washed my face. I didn't have time for self-pity or for obsessing about Max. I had a job to do and my break time was over. Time to get back to work.

Later in the afternoon, I got an email from my boss. He wanted to meet at four o'clock today. Was it about the presentation? Or something else entirely? I didn't feel good about it.

When I reached my boss's office at the scheduled time, I was surprised to see Max already there. It wasn't just Max; his supervisor, Sean, stood by the desk. Maybe we were being congratulated on a job well done on the presentation, but if so, where was Amica and Jon?

I could tell by the frowns and the nervous glances Max gave me that it wasn't going to be good. Dread pooled in my stomach. I squeezed my hands together to keep them from shaking. This was bad on so many levels.

Ben ushered me in, and I sat in the only chair available next to Max. He gave me a nervous smile before looking forward again. Ben walked over to the front of the desk. He glanced over at Sean and motioned for him to go first.

"As you both know there is a company policy against romantic relationships between coworkers."

How did they know? My heart tried to jump out of my chest. I was sure I was about to lose my lunch. And my job. We'd been so careless.

"Chase and I aren't dating," Max said. "You guys have nothing to worry about."

Ben shook his head. "We're not idiots," he said. "We could tell the minute you two got together. First of all, Chase was more social in the last month than he's been since he got here. He's been sitting with new people. Smiling. Engaging."

"Max, we can see a lot of changes in you, too," Sean said.

"Less pranks. Less getting in trouble, although it did seem like the copier was getting a lot of use."

Max was shaking his head when I put a hand on his arm. "If what you're saying is true," I said. "Why didn't you say anything about it weeks ago? The changes that you listed were positive not negative."

"You're right," Sean said. "That's exactly why we didn't say anything."

"We should have, though." Ben stepped forward, crossing his arms. "We turned a blind eye, and that was probably a mistake. But I'm going to be honest with you guys, and if you repeat this, I'll deny this conversation ever happened. You guys are two of our best. I'd hate to lose either of you. And, honestly you seemed happier." He looked over at Sean. "We were just going to ignore it."

"Maybe that makes us bad supervisors," Sean said. "Company rules are company rules, after all. But because you were working so well together on this project, we thought maybe it would work out."

"But we were wrong," Ben said. "There are reasons dating is not allowed. Not necessarily because of the happy times. It's because most of the time, it doesn't work out, and then you have two people who can't work together."

"We can work together," I said.

"Like you did today?"

"Wait a minute," Max interrupted. "I was a little distracted. I'm not gonna lie about that, but we did well. Our presentation was good."

"No one is saying it wasn't. But there's a strain now that wasn't there before, and now it's becoming more obvious. Obvious to everyone, not just us, and now we have to do something."

I sat up straighter in the chair. "But I don't understand. If

Max and I are no longer dating, there shouldn't be a problem. Wouldn't the first step be to ask us not to date? Done."

"If this was the end of it, we might have let it go. Honestly, it's not the first time we've seen people get together and break up so quickly it was barely worth mentioning. Especially when they could still work together or just not ever talk to each other again. You guys aren't even the same unit and you have different supervisors."

I bristled at his comment about our relationship being barely worth mentioning. It was so much more than that. At least for me. I didn't say any of that. "So, what's the problem?"

"The problem is I can see the way you guys look at each other. This isn't going away. Tell me right now you guys are done, and that this won't happen again, and we can walk out of this room and go on with their lives."

I started to say something, but Sean held up his hand. "I want to hear from Max first."

I glanced at Max, my breath catching in my throat. I didn't know what to wish for. If Max said we were done, it would save both our jobs. But it might just break my heart. Our gazes caught for a second and then Max faced his boss.

"Being with Chase was the best thing that ever happened to me. I can always find another job. Right now, Chase wants nothing to do with me, but I can't promise that I won't try every day for the rest of my life to get him back."

"Max," I said, but my ability to form words ended there. What did I say to that? I knew it was a problem. It could cost us our jobs, but I couldn't hold back the warmth that spread like wildfire in my chest. Did Max really care about me that much?

"That's what I thought." Sean pulled a chair out and straddled it, facing us. "What do we do now, guys?" Ben moved behind his desk.

Were they doing a good-cop, bad-cop thing? I shook my head. I didn't have an answer for them.

"What are our options?" Max asked.

"Option number one is that we ask one of you to leave." Sean leaned on the chair as he talked. It could have been a casual conversation, except for the subject matter and Ben glowering in the background.

"Quit?" I bit my lip to keep from saying anything more. The thought of quitting... Of trying to go somewhere new, terrified me.

"No," Ben said. "Just moving to another office. We have a call center across town."

Even transferring to another area scared me. I wasn't sure I could do it. But the thought of Max leaving terrified me more. What if I never saw him again? I couldn't even think about it.

"We also have the sales unit on the seventh floor. Even though we're technically the same company, you'd be working in a different division, so you can do that and still date."

"Is there another option?" I asked.

"I think if you guys were back together, and we didn't know about it, no harm, no foul. That would mean not using the copy room to make out. If there's no drama on the floor, I think we'd be good." Sean glanced back at Ben. "Did I miss anything?"

"Nope."

"I'd like to go with the first option," Max said. Everyone stared at him, including me.

"Seriously?" I couldn't believe he was willing to let one of us leave instead of getting back together. I thought Max had wanted us to be together. Had I once again got it wrong?

"Explain," said Sean.

"Just so we're clear. I want to get back together with Chase. But I don't want him to be pressured into doing that just so we can keep our jobs, especially since it might not be what he wants. And if someone has to move, I want it to be me." Max stared straight ahead, never looking at me. "Chase doesn't like change, so I would never put him in a situation where he had to move. I started this whole thing. It's my fault." He turned to look at me then, his eyes full of emotion. "I should be the one to leave."

I shook my head. I wasn't sure what I was even saying no to: Max leaving or that it was all his fault.

"We just wanted you guys to be aware of what was going on."

"The whole *you know that we know* thing," Ben added.

"Exactly. We don't want to do anything right now, but we need to be thinking about it because if we're noticing, other people are noticing. We may be forced into a decision."

"And we want you guys to be a part of that decision as much as possible," Ben said. "Are we clear?"

"Not really." I was lost. Were they asking us to do something or not?

"We're clear," Max said. He stood up and held out his hand for me. I didn't even hesitate. I put my hand in his and let him pull me up. I wanted to pull Max into a hug, but I wasn't ready yet. I wasn't ready to just forgive and forget.

"Why don't we take a week and see how it goes? We can always decide something if we need to."

"Come on, Chase," Max said. "Let's go."

Ben and Sean were conversing by the window. They were clearly done with us.

We walked out to the small area next to the sups offices. "Max," I said. "You didn't have to do that."

"I meant everything I said in there." Max touched the side of my face, pushing a stray strand of hair behind my ear before walking away. I was more confused than ever.

That night I did something I swore I'd never do. I called Cameron.

"Hey, Chase. How are you?" His voice sounded so familiar and so foreign at the same time.

"Good. Is there any way we can meet? Just to talk?"

Cameron hesitated and I worried he was going to say no. "Sure. Just tell me when and where.

"Tonight. At seven. I'll text you the address."

My sister called while I was getting ready. "Really can't talk right now," I said.

"I'm meeting someone in an hour, and I need to get ready."

"Max?" Her voice sounded hopeful. I almost didn't tell her. She would be disappointed and not just that it wasn't Max. "No, not Max. Cameron." It was like a Band-Aid. Sometimes you had to just rip it off.

"Chase, are you crazy?"

"I can't talk about it right now. Okay? I'll tell you about it later but right now, I need to get ready." I hung up on her before she could say another word. Ignoring would work for now, but not for long. She wouldn't give up.

But was I doing the right thing?

NINETEEN

Max

I TRIED TO IGNORE THE BANGING on my apartment door. I'd had a tough day, and I just wanted to curl up next to my dog and watch reruns of *Gilligan's Island*. Was that too much to ask? I'd almost lost my job today. I'd already lost my boyfriend. What else could happen? The look on Chase's face during the meeting had given me the slightest hope, but I was afraid of getting rejected again. What if Chase still didn't want me?

I probably could've ignored the banging, but I couldn't ignore Toby, who was barking furiously at the door and making so much noise I was sure the neighbors would be calling soon. Mrs. Davis was not my biggest fan, and losing my apartment on top of everything else would be devastating. Especially for Toby. Adjusting to new places had never been easy for him.

The banging reminded me I still needed to answer the door. Whoever it was—they were persistent and not likely to be deterred by me pretending I wasn't home. I had no choice but to answer it. As I pulled on my sleep pants, I had the slightest hope, very slight, that it was Chase. If I didn't answer it, I wouldn't have to face that disappointment. And if it was him? I was making the man wait. That more than anything had me heading for the door.

I sighed as I picked up my maniac dog before reaching for the door. "Tobias, calm down," I said as I turned the knob. I almost dropped my poor dog in surprise when I saw the person who'd been waiting impatiently for me to answer.

"Sunny?"

"Can I come in?" she asked. "There's some old lady wandering the hallway." Without waiting for a reply, she pushed past me.

"Of course." I shut the door, trying to hold on to my squirming dog. Finally, I gave up and put him down. Toby ran up to her, barking ferociously. "Don't take it personally," I said. "He sees everyone as a threat, including the vacuum."

She leaned down and let him smell her hand. "What a cute little dog. Tobias?"

"Toby, actually."

She petted his head and stroked his ear before standing back up. Toby wagged his tail, deciding she was not a threat. I wasn't so sure.

"What the hell did you do my brother?" Sunny glared at me.

"Would you like some coffee or tea? Or one of Toby's sedatives?"

"Coffee is fine," she said. "We might as well be civil about this."

I prepared the coffee, a little nervous about turning my back on her. I moved sideways so I could see her and the coffee at the same time. "Did you come to exterminate me?"

"Nothing is off the table, as of yet."

"Thanks for your honesty." I placed the cups on the table

and sat across from her. She didn't seem threatening, and Toby had deemed her safe. But the memory of our previous conversation on how she could kill me and get away with it was at the forefront of my mind. I kept my coffee close so she couldn't slip anything in my cup.

"Tell me what you did."

"It's really between me and your brother."

"It's really not." She stared at me, waiting. There was no way I was going to win this, but I had to try.

"Sunny, you know Chase hates it when people invade his privacy and take away his power. You have to respect that."

"I do," she said, stirring sugar into her coffee. "That's why I haven't been here before now. That and I was researching ways to kill you. Kidding." She smiled and I wasn't sure she was. "Mostly."

"Why are you here now?"

"Chase's privacy no longer matters to me. Not when he's going out with Cameron."

My mouth dropped open, and I quickly shut it again. Adrenaline coursed through me. "Chase is going out with Cameron?"

"That's what I said."

"Why would he do that? The man was a complete ass to him." I put my cup down before I threw it across the room. The anger was a surprise, but the jealousy...someone else touching, kissing, my Chase, that was expected. Those thoughts of losing Chase to someone else had kept me company for the last week.

"That's what I'm asking you. What did you do that was so bad that Chase would run back to his ex-boyfriend who is a total douche?"

The guilt was never far behind. I had done this. "He didn't tell you anything?"

"He told me you were a jerk. An ass. And he had some other colorful words to describe you. You want to go into those too?"

"No. I get the picture." I sighed, resigned. "Chase is my competitor at work. I couldn't figure out how he always got a better customer service rating than I did."

"Because he's better than you."

"Obviously. You want to hear this or not?"

She nodded for me to go on.

"I used my brother-in-law's account to call in as a customer so I could figure out how he was getting such great ratings."

"That's horrible."

I ignored her statement. "What I found surprised me; Chase wasn't the cold bitchy guy that he pretended to be." I glanced up at her, wanting her to believe me. "And I realized I wanted to know this guy better. I tried to talk to him, but he was very resistant." I shrugged. "I have a bit of a reputation as a player."

"Earned?"

"Totally. Chase was smart not to talk to me." I stared at my cup. I was glad to finally be able to talk to someone about this, but it was still difficult. "I'd had a taste of what the real Chase was like, and I wanted more. I called again under my brother-in-law's name."

Her mouth dropped open. "So, you're the guy?"

"What are you talking about?"

"Chase told me about a customer who called in. He said just talking to the guy made him want to be in a relationship. It reminded him of what he could have. Right after that, he started talking to you?"

"Yes." I thought back. "I think it was right after that he started giving me a chance."

"You did that, Max."

My chest warmed up. Just by talking to me, Chase wanted to give love a chance. That was kind of amazing."

"And then you destroyed it."

"Hey," I said. "You don't even know what happened."

"I can guess. Chase found out what you did. I just don't know the how."

"I introduced him to my family—including my brother-in-law." I shook my head. I still couldn't believe I was such an idiot.

"And you weren't prepared for that? You didn't realize that could happen? Seriously?"

"I'm an idiot okay? I get it. I was just so madly in love, I didn't think of it."

"You love him?"

"I really should have told him first and not you."

"Too late." She smiled. "It's not like I didn't know already. You guys are perfect for each other."

"I thought you wanted to kill me."

"I do. But mostly because you're screwing this up, and Chase is dating his ex-boyfriend again." She put down her coffee and focused all her attention on me. "You have to get him back."

"Do you have any suggestions?"

"Do I have to do all the work?" She tilted her head. "Think, Max. How did you win him the first time? Maybe try that again."

Long after she left, I thought about what she'd said. I had to do something. Waiting for Chase to decide what he wanted was no longer an option. There was no way I could let him go back to that jerk. Except, of course, I would if that's what Chase really wanted. First, I had to find out what Chase wanted. If there was even a chance I could get him back, I was going for it. But I had to do it before it was too late.

Sunny had given me an idea. Even though I was

pretending to be someone else, I was more myself and more honest when I was talking to Chase on the phone.

Looks like my brother-in-law was going to make another service call.

TWENTY
Chase

I DRUMMED MY FINGERS ON THE TABLE as I waited. I'd gotten a table in the corner away from the crowds. I didn't like being out in public, but I couldn't do this in private. The longer I sat there waiting, the more convinced I was that it was a mistake. I stood up to leave when I spotted Cameron walking through the door. He was tall and gorgeous, just like always. A man who captured everyone's attention the minute he walked in the room. I waved him over, and he kissed my cheek in greeting. The familiar ache I'd had around him in the past was gone. Now he was just a pretty man to admire from afar. Not that I'd even be doing that. I thought of Max and the ache returned. Only it was deeper than I'd ever experienced with my ex.

"Chase, so good to see you." He sat down across from me. "I was surprised to get your call. Actually, shocked is a more accurate word." Cameron's words seemed to carry across the room. It wasn't that he was talking loudly, it was just the way his deep voice commanded attention. Just like Max.

I smiled at him, no longer annoyed by the attention Cameron brought on us. It didn't seem to be at all purposeful.

It was just the way he was. Had I really expected Cameron to change? "It's nice to see you, too."

After we ordered our drinks, Cameron shifted in his chair, not meeting my eyes. Was he nervous? "I am glad to be here"—he cleared his throat—"but I feel I should tell you I'm with someone now."

I laughed, causing him to glance up, a frown on his face. "I'm sorry," I said. "I didn't mean to laugh. I'm happy for you, Cam. I just..." I shook my head. "I'm not here to try and get you back."

"Of course not," he said. He took a deep breath and finally met my gaze. "Why are we here?"

My smile faded. Could I really do this? Could I really ask Cameron the questions I had? "Let's eat first. Then I'll explain everything."

The waiter arrived to take our order. Cameron went first and then turned to me. I didn't hesitate. Ordering quickly was something I'd worked on with Max. There was no wrong answer. Max never made fun of me, so I didn't feel under pressure. It helped that I didn't care what Cameron thought. I flirted a little with the waiter. Not that he was gay. It was obvious he wasn't, but I'd learned from Max that treating everyone as if we were all in on some big secret together won them over.

When I glanced back at Cameron, he was staring at me. "Is my eye liner off? I've started wearing it to highlight the color of my eyes. Ma—" I stopped there. I didn't want to talk about Max. Although, really, it was inevitable.

"You've changed." Cameron watched me closely as if seeing me for the first time. "You're more confident. Less afraid."

"Oh, I'm still as anxious as you remember. I'm just working on overcoming it as best I can. In the most comfortable way I can."

"It looks good on you, Chase."

"The eyeliner?"

"The confidence."

"Oh." I blushed. "Thank you."

We ate our meals, talking about our jobs, friends we used to have, and our families. I finished more of my meal than I expected. I was nervous. Not just about asking Cameron the questions I had but about the answers I might get. Would it be helpful or was I wasting both of our time? It was good to see him. Even if just to close that part of my life for good.

"So why are we here, Chase?"

I stretched out my fingers to release my nervous energy. "I wanted to talk about what happened with us."

A flash of anger crossed Cameron's face. "It's about two years too late."

"I know." I sighed. "It wasn't fair of me to leave like that. I realize that now." I again thought of Max. But I had let Max explain. Maybe not right away, but at least I didn't wait two years."

The anger left as soon as it appeared, and Cameron sighed. "Why now?"

"I met someone too," I said softly. "It didn't work out. I'm wondering if I could have done anything..." I stared at the liquid in my drink. The bubbles in the soda migrated to the top. I wanted to be more like those bubbles, rising to the top instead of always falling to the bottom. Mostly I didn't want to see the pity or God forbid, the gloating in Cam's eyes.

"Chase. Please look at me."

I lifted my eyes reluctantly. All I saw in his eyes was compassion. "I'm sorry. Do you want to talk about it?"

"Am I self-centered?"

Cameron laughed. "Is that what he told you?" At my glare he held up his hand. "Sorry. We're all a bit self-centered, Chase. We see everything from our own experiences. It's not that we can't think of others. I'm not saying that. It's just we have a thing called self-preservation. Sometimes that keeps us from taking chances or wanting to see from someone else's perspective. You and I were complete opposites. It was never going to work out."

He was right. But what did that say about Max and me? Was there any chance? I blinked back the tears threatening to fall.

"But opposites also attract," Cameron said. "I honestly believe that opposites can complement each other."

"You're just saying that."

"I mean it, Chase." He pulled out his phone and smiled as he scrolled through it. When he found what he wanted, he turned the screen to me. It was a picture of a sweet guy with a shy smile. "This is my boyfriend, Paul."

It wasn't at all what I expected. "He's very cute."

"We're complete opposites. But he makes me better. And I do the same for him. It wasn't because we were opposites that we didn't work out, Chase. We weren't right for each other. I'm not saying I didn't love you. I did. It's just not the same..."

"I know." And I did. I didn't care for Cameron the way I did for Max.

"And if your guy is the reason for the changes I see in you, then I think you should give him another chance."

"You think I needed to change?" The bitterness over our relationship and how I was never good enough for Cameron was still there, somewhere inside me. Would I ever be able to let that go?

"No," he said, taking my hand. "Change isn't really the right word. You're just a better version of yourself. You're confident and happy. That's the difference, Chase."

"I don't feel happy."

"Don't give up on love. No matter how scary it is." He squeezed my hand and then let go.

I didn't want to talk about it anymore. Thinking of Max just made me sad and frustrated. "Tell me about your guy," I said.

It worked. Cameron talked about Paul and how happy they were. I was a little jealous. Not of Paul, but of what they had. Was that possible for Max and me? Could I ever trust him again? I had a lot to think about but that would be later when I was alone.

Cameron insisted on paying even though dinner was my idea. As we stood up to leave, Cam touched my hand again. "I wanted to tell you how sorry I am. I realized later, after my pride recovered, and a little processing that I didn't always respect what you wanted. I thought you were being overly dramatic. That you acted that way to frustrate me. I realize now how hard it was for you. Talk about being self-centered." He gave a self-deprecating laugh, shaking his head. "Please don't judge this guy based on what happened with us."

I hugged Cameron, surprising us both. "Thank you," I whispered.

Later, back at home, I thought of Max, and processed the things Cameron had said. I wanted to trust Max again, but I didn't know how. Were we really right for each other or would it all just fall apart again? I fell asleep to thoughts of Max and how much I missed him.

The next day, I still hadn't figured out what to do. I tried turning my brain off for a while. Maybe if I just didn't think about it for a day or two, my path would seem clearer. Turning off my brain wasn't the hardest part. I was able to focus on work and the customers and figuring out the specific problem each one had. No, it was my heart that was the problem. My eyes strayed toward Max's cubicle even though I couldn't see him from mine. I missed him. I'd become attached to him in such a short amount of time. But I felt like I'd known Max forever. Which was crazy. Okay, so maybe my brain wasn't cooperating either. Another phone call distracted me from my moping.

At lunch, I decided to go to the breakroom. Ignoring Max wasn't helping me at all. I had to get back to normal at some point. I sat down beside Amica.

"Hey, stranger." She grinned at me. I realized I missed hanging out with her.

We chatted about work. Thankfully, she didn't mention Max at all. I was glad to talk to my friend again. Why had I sequestered myself away? My eyes strayed every once in a while toward the door.

"I saw Max and Dylan leaving when I first got here."

"That's nice," I said, trying and utterly failing to sound like I didn't care. Amica didn't call me on it. She really was a good friend.

I thought I spotted Max when I took my afternoon break. I needed a soda to keep myself focused. He was walking away from me. Was it a metaphor for something? Or just the way it needed to be? Still, maybe if I could have seen his eyes, it would have helped. Every time I passed by signs on the copy room, storage room, and snack room, it made me smile. I thought of Max and making out with him.

I was about to sign out for the day when another call came through. It didn't matter when my shift ended; if we got a call, we had to take it. Not that I really minded. I had an empty apartment to go to.

"Hello, this is Chase from Coxx Communications. Can I have your name and account number please?"

"Hi, Chase." The voice at the other end of the line was familiar. Very familiar and I wasn't sure how I'd missed it before. “My account is under the name Howard Hernandez.” He rattled off the number.

I placed my hand over my pounding heart, trying to calm down. “How can I help you?”

“I’ve broken something, and I’m not sure how to fix it.”

TWENTY-ONE

Max

CHASE HADN'T HUNG UP. I took that as a good sign. I wasn't sure what I expected him to do. Maybe scream and yell at me? I was taking a chance by calling again. If I lost my job, I could find another. But it would be devastating for Chase. I almost chickened out several times for that reason, but the thought of Chase going back to Cameron was enough to steel my resolve.

"Let me see if I can help you with that," Chase said. "Your account looks fine. Can you tell me more about what's broken?"

Was there a hint of amusement in his voice? "Everything." I sighed. How was I going to do this without both of us losing our jobs? "Nothing's working for me anymore. I fucked up." I thought I heard a quickly stifled laugh. "I just need help fixing it again."

"So, it's your fault. Is that what you're saying?"

"It was fine before I touched it." I halted those thoughts. I couldn't think about touching Chase or I'd never get through this. "And now it's broken."

"Well, is it really just one person's fault?" Chase said.

My heart beat faster. Was he giving me a chance? "It is my fault. I'm sorry I messed up." I hoped he'd hear me. This might be my only chance to apologize.

"But you're willing to fix it?"

"I'll do whatever it takes, Chase." Hope made me giddy. Would he really give me a chance?

"And how will you keep from breaking it again? How would you keep from making the same mistakes over and over?"

I could hear the seriousness in Chase's voice. This was an important question for him. "I know what I did wrong."

"What was that?"

He surprised me with the question. I couldn't just spit it out. Not when anyone could listen in. "I didn't respect...the technology," I said.

"And now you do?"

"Yes. And I'll do anything to make it right."

"I'm not sure if it's something we can fix," Chase said, and my heart plummeted. "Not here and now, anyway."

"Maybe you could send someone over. Someone who can show me how to do it the right way."

"And if there's no one available?"

"I'll come to you. Just tell me when and where, and what you want me to do." I swallowed the tightness in my throat. "Chase, I think you're the only one that can help me."

"I'm just not sure," he said. "I may have to call you back."

I didn't want to end the call. Just hearing Chase's voice again filled my heart with joy. What if I never got to talk to him again? I couldn't risk another call. This was it. This was my final chance. If this didn't work, I had to let Chase go. "Thank you for your help," I said. "I appreciate you. I want you to know that."

"Thank you...Mr. Hernandez."

I laughed and said goodbye one final time before hanging up. We had a chance. Now it was all up to Chase.

By the next day, that hope was dwindling. I expected Chase to call last night or maybe stop by. I checked my phone at least a hundred times to make sure I didn't have it on mute or had accidentally missed his call, but there was nothing. Toby seemed to sense my restlessness. He barked at everything, even the TV.

And by Friday, I'd convinced myself that it was over. Nothing I could do would bring Chase back to me.

I ignored all my friends. Dylan, Sadie, even Amica had all tried to talk to me. My stomach was in knots. Was this really the way it was going to be?

I finished my call, scooting my chair back. It hadn't gone well. I couldn't focus. I glanced up and noticed Chase standing in front of my desk, looking gorgeous as ever. His long, blond hair framing his face. But it was the half smile on his face that made my heart race. He didn't say a word. He raised an eyebrow up and slipped a note on my desk. I didn't even look at the note. I watched Chase turn and walk away, his hips swaying.

When I couldn't see him any longer, I picked up the note, remembering the last one I got from him. I smiled as I opened it up.

> Appointment Reminder for Howard Hernandez (AKA Max): Tonight-7:00 p.m. Your Place. Be prepared to grovel.

"What's that?" Dylan asked, rolling himself over.

"Redemption." I showed him the note.

"This time," he said with a smile. "Don't heck it up."

❦

Chase arrived right on time, wearing the same clothes he wore the first time we met, all the way down to his sexy black boots. I immediately wanted to rip them off him. I stared at him for a good minute.

"Well, are you gonna let me in?" His voice was sassy, and I resisted the urge to kiss him until he promised to never leave again.

I invited him in. Toby, the traitor, barely barked at him. Instead, he scrambled around his legs, wagging his tail.

Chase laughed with genuine joy as he picked up the small dog. "Hey there, Toboroni. I missed you so much, buddy." He kissed him on the head. There was no reason to be jealous of my dog but at that moment, I was. Chase set the dog down and took a step toward me. "Did someone call for a technician?"

"Are you here to fix what I broke?" Our eyes locked. My pulse raced at his nearness. I wanted to touch him.

"No, I'm here to help us figure out how we can move past this. Maybe work together to keep it fixed?"

"So you're taking me back?"

"Only if you stop talking right now and kiss me."

"Done." I pulled him into a kiss, holding him tightly as I explored his mouth. Chase moaned.

"I missed you so much."

"Me, too, babe." I tangled my hand in his hair, pulling his head back to kiss his neck. "I know there are things we need to talk about."

"Later," Chase said. "We can talk about rules and boundaries and not stepping all over each other, but right now I only want to get into this." He slid his hand down below the waistband of my pants and squeezed my ass.

"You have all the best plans." I started undressing him, undoing each button on his shirt to expose his firm chest and slim waist. "Don't worry, I'll give you a good rating."

Chase laughed. "I always aim to please."

I led him to the bedroom, ignoring Toby's whine as I shut the door. "Sorry, Tobes," I said, "he's mine tonight."

"And every night," Chase added, pulling me over to the bed.

We undressed quickly. I missed everything about him. His smell. His taste. I couldn't get enough. He was lying on his back, staring up at me. "Chase," I said. "Let me take care of you. I know you like to take control, but tonight I want to make you feel good."

He nodded, his eyes bright with tears. "I'd like that."

"I love you, Chase."

"I know."

I laughed. I didn't need to hear the words yet. I could tell by the look in his eyes. I kissed him deeply, before trailing kisses down his neck. I licked and sucked at his skin. His nipples peaked as I took each one into my mouth. He groaned, arching his back. I continued exploring down his abs to the light blond hair that trailed down to his cock. I teased him before taking him into my mouth.

"Max," he cried out, threading his fingers through my hair and guiding my head. I could tell he was getting close already by the way he was tensing up.

"I've got you, babe. Just let go."

"Wait," he said, panting. "Don't want to come yet, Max. I want you inside me."

We'd never done that before. Chase always wanted to be the one on top. "Are you sure?"

"I trust you." He pulled me up for a kiss. "I love you, Max."

"I know," I said with a wink. And I did, but hearing lit up something inside me. I grabbed the lube and condoms from my nightstand. I watched his face for any signs he'd changed his mind as I prepared him. His skin was flushed with desire, and red marks stood out from where my stubble had scratched him. He was stunning, and I was so lucky to have him.

"Anytime today." He pushed back against my fingers. "I want your cock now, Maxwell."

"Yes, sir," I said. 'You're the boss." I pushed into him, letting him adjust, before my balls slapped against his ass.

"Move."

I pulled out and slammed back into him. He felt so good. I didn't usually top, but with Chase I wanted to give him whatever he needed. We soon were both panting and ready.

"Not going to last," he said. His eyes were screwed tight and his breathing shallow.

"Come for me, babe."

That's all it took. I came soon after he did, pulling out gently and tying off the condom. I got up and retrieved a warm washcloth. He watched me as I took care of him.

"Don't ever leave me."

"Never," I said.

We cleaned up and snuggled on the couch. Toby settled between us, happy to finally get some attention. We watched some stupid comedy that made Chase laugh. His giggles reached in and grabbed a hold of my heart. I never wanted to be without him. How did I ever think going from guy to guy was the best thing to do? I was no longer worried I'd get bored of Chase or the life we had. That would never happen. He was all I wanted. All I would ever want.

TWENTY-TWO

Chase

EPILOGUE

MAKE-UP SEX WAS THE BEST SEX EVER. It had been two weeks since I showed up at Max's apartment, and we were still making up. Surely, it would fade a little. I talked to Max about throwing in an argument here and there so we could make up again. Max said we could argue as much as I wanted as long as I never left him. I happily agreed.

We had dinner again with Max's family. I apologized for leaving so quickly. No one blamed me, and the story became legendary. They all enjoyed the retelling of it. It didn't bother me anymore. I thought it was funny. I was able to take down the great Max Sloan. The girls at the office and probably some of the guys were heartbroken. They thought they had a chance.

We also had dinner with my sister and her family. She no longer wanted to murder Max in his sleep. At times I thought she might like him even better than me. But I still had my adoring nieces. Most of the time. If Max wasn't around.

The only downside was worrying over what to do about work. Most of the time, it was great. I had lunch with Max, Dylan, and Amica, and although the participants varied depending on when we'd get our lunch break, I could engage with others even if Max wasn't there. I had more confidence in myself. The doubt about my anxiety that I always attributed to Cameron, right or wrong, was mostly gone. It would never be fully gone. It was part of the disorder. I was happy most days, although I still had some bad days. Max took care of me. Never making me feel less because of it.

The reality didn't hit us until we received an email from Ben and Sean. They scheduled a meeting for us to meet with them at four today. I wasn't sure what to do. It was obvious to everyone we were back together. They'd insinuated we could stay if we were together, but I wasn't sure if that was true. Max talked about transferring to sales. He didn't want us to have that constant worry that we could be fired at any time. He was right, but I hated the idea of him not being there. It was only a few floors up, which was definitely better than across town. And exponentially better than either of us having to quit. My stomach twisted in knots as I walked with Max to Sean's office.

The door was shut when we got there.

"Should we knock?" There was an unwritten rule about not bothering their bosses if the door was closed. They were usually on a conference call or meeting with employees or some other activity they didn't want interrupted. As far as I knew this rule went for every single boss in their department, but I couldn't be sure since we'd always had Sean and Ben as our bosses. Workers came and went from the company, but the bosses usually stayed the same.

Max shrugged. "We have an appointment."

"True, true." I knocked at the door softly at first but then harder when no one answered. We heard some scuffling like a chair hitting the wall. We looked at each other again.

The door suddenly flew open. Ben stood there, slightly

disheveled. I couldn't put my finger on it exactly. He just wasn't as put together as normal.

"Gentlemen," he said, sounding composed. "Thank you for joining us."

Sean stood by the desk, holding a file in front of him. My heart rate tripled. What did he have? Was it transcripts of the calls Max had made to him? Was it transfer forms? Were we about to get fired? My eyes darted back to Max, but he seemed calm. His eyes narrowed as if he was trying to figure something out. His hand rested on my back, helping me not freak out. Maybe he shouldn't be touching me in front of them, but I figured they already knew something was going on. And I needed the support. His touch grounded me. Max was there no matter what happened. We would get through this. Together.

We sat down in the chairs. Ben and Sean looked at each other as if they weren't sure how to start. At least they didn't appear to have their minds made up or maybe they just weren't sure how to say it.

"Are we fired?" I didn't know why I blurted that out. If they didn't have the idea in their head, why would I want to give it to them?

"What?" Sean said, with a laugh. "Of course not."

"Should you be fired?" Ben stepped over to stand next to his counterpart.

"Just excuse my friend here. He's a little nervous." Max gave me a warm look.

"Things have been going well over the last couple weeks," Ben said. "That gives me some hope." He looked at Sean and then focused once again on us. "Are you guys back together?"

I started to say something when Max put his hand on my arm.

"Before we answer that, we need to get something straight," Max said. "Is this conversation confidential? Or will it be used against us? Because, honestly, I'll say whatever it is you need me to say."

"We're not recording this." Ben held out his hands. "I guess I'd like a little of both. Honesty is appreciated, but we also need to tow the company line. Does that make sense?"

"Not really," I said.

Ben hesitated and glanced over at Sean.

Sean stepped forward, putting the file on the desk. I still couldn't figure out what was in the file and if he was going to use it against us. "We like you guys," Sean said. "You're fantastic workers. You get the job done and usually with a minimal amount of trouble. In the last several months, we've had a problem not only with staff turnover, but with the amount of drama on the floor. That's why we've had to enforce the no-relationship policy." He glanced at Ben who quickly looked away. "If I'm being honest, and this is something I would deny later if asked, I don't care if you guys are dating. What I care about is you doing the job and doing it well. You guys usually make our job easier. We've got plenty of problem employees to deal with. And your worker retention project is exactly what we wanted." He sighed. "We don't want to lose either of you guys, but we can't turn away and ignore a blatant disregard for policy. We just can't do that because if we let you guys get away with it, then other people are going to do it, and we'll have more problems."

"So, we can't date."

"No, Chase. That's not what we're saying."

"That's exactly what we're saying," Ben interrupted. "Officially."

I looked from one to the other, confused. What were they saying?

"Let me be perfectly clear." Sean stepped forward, glancing back at Ben before facing us. "What happens between you guys is none of our business unless it affects the work that you do. Or unless it's so blatantly obvious that other people are noticing, and we have no choice but to act. Do you understand?"

"I get it."

"What that means," Ben said. "Is no making out in the copy room."

"No holding hands or kissing at work." Sean crossed his arms.

"We can spend our breaks together? Lunch together?"

"You guys are friends, right? No problem," Sean said. "But if you guys have a rough spot in your *friendship*"—he actually used air quotes around the word—"and ignore each other when you come to work, that's fine. We just can't have a loss of production. We can't have fights or arguing."

"We can't have people calling and pretending to be other people," Ben added with a pointed look at Max.

Shit! I sneaked a glance at Max, but he looked innocent, like he had no idea what they were talking about. Okay. I could do this.

"Do you get what we're saying here?" Sean stared at Max.

"Yes, absolutely," Max said. "Chase and I are friends and we might disagree now and then but we won't bring it to work."

"Perfect." Ben smiled at us both.

"So, no one is getting fired?" It seemed too good to be true. I wanted to be sure.

"Not today." Sean nodded at them.

That nod meant we were being dismissed. I couldn't wait to get out of the office before they changed their minds. When I reached the door, I glanced back. Sean was in a whispered conversation with Ben. We had already been forgotten.

"Excuse me," I said. They both looked up, surprised to see us still there. "Do you want the door open or shut?"

"Definitely shut."

I did as he asked and looked over at Max. "Well, that was weird."

"I can't believe it," Max said. "I was totally prepared to go in there and sign any transfer papers they had."

"And now you don't have to go." I wanted to kiss him, but that was definitely on the Don't Do At Work list.

"We better get back to work. I'll see you later, babe." He squeezed my hand.

The rest of the day rushed by, and I was happier than I had for a long time. I had a job I loved. A man I loved. And now I'd get to keep both. I walked over to Max's desk after my last call. He was still on a call, so I waited patiently by the desk as other workers filed out. Several of them smiled at me and wished me a good night. I smiled in return. Had it only been a few months ago when no one would talk to me? And I had been afraid to talk to them. So much had changed and although I was the one who'd actually changed, I gave Max all the credit. He helped me feel safe and secure and loved. He helped me build confidence in myself. He didn't treat me as if I were defective. I would never be the outgoing social butterfly Max was. That was never going to happen. But I no longer had to shrink away and hide from everyone.

Max was still on the call. It didn't matter how long it took; we had to finish a call. Even if it ran an hour over. Most of the workers had already left. The office had an evening shift, but it was much smaller than the day shift. Silence filled the office except for Max's voice. Most of the cubicles were empty. I sat in Dylan's chair and turned in circles, making myself dizzy. Max was agreeing to something and saying that he could send a tech out if needed. He shook his head at me with a smile on his face.

Sean passed by, his eyebrows raised. I stopped twirling. That was probably on the stop doing list, too. "Just waiting for my friend to get done," I said, not even using the air quotes. "He's my ride." I leaned over the desk to watch him walk away. I wanted to see if he was leaving the building. Instead of going right toward the elevators, Sean turned left and went into the copy room and closed the door. That was weird. Of course, he was a sup so he could just ignore the big sign on the door.

"Thank you very much, ma'am for calling Coxx Communications. Please stay on the line to take a short survey about the service you received today."

Max hung up and shook his head. "People over ninety shouldn't be left alone with technology."

I laughed. "What happened?"

"I tried to get her to enter a password, and she couldn't figure out why the letters she was entering were turning into dots." Max shook his head. "She kept deleting them over and over. I asked if she had anyone who could help her, and she said she did have one friend, but they weren't talking to each other right now. So, I offered to send out a tech."

I couldn't help but laugh, even though I could tell Max was still irritated by the call. "You do a great job," I said, kissing him on the cheek.

Someone cleared their throat behind us. Oops. Ben was still the building.

"Just a friendly kiss among friends," I said, gathering my stuff as Max pulled me toward the elevators.

"Are you leaving for the night?" Max asked him.

"No, I still..." He cleared his throat again. "I have some things to finish up."

"Okay, well, have a good weekend."

"You guys have a good one, too."

When we reached the elevators, I glanced back at Ben. He paused in front of the door to the copy room and listened for a minute. Then he went inside.

"Is there something going on with Ben and Sean?"

"I don't know, and I don't care," Max said. "I have my own man to worry about.

Once we were alone in the elevator, I kissed him lightly on the lips.

"We're in public. At work."

"I'm a rule breaker." I shrugged.

"Chase Corrigan? A rule breaker?" he teased. "Since when?"

"Since you." I wrapped my arms around him, pulling him into a kiss that lasted until the elevator dinged. "I could definitely get used to this."

Max grinned as he grabbed my hand and pulled me toward the parking garage. "Heck and heck yeah."

What are Ben and Sean doing in the copy room? For a free short, click here. Interested in Ben and Sean's story? Look for Message Received, a prequel to Talk to Me, coming July 2022.

DEAR READERS,

Thank you for reading Talk to Me. It's the first book in the Sloan Brothers series. I enjoyed writing this story. I appreciate those who shared their experiences living with anxiety. It's a disorder that is common but greatly misunderstood.

I also loved sharing Toby with you. He is part of our family and actually does bark at everyone and everything, including the vacuum. He also has a nervous licking habit.

Next up is Ben and Sean's story, Message Received, a prequel to Talk to Me. Ben believes in structure and planning and following the rules which is a problem when it comes to his gorgeous and totally off-limits new employee. Can Sean break through the walls Ben has around him?

You can follow me on Amazon to find out about new releases and follow me on my Facebook page to get sneak peeks of stories to come.

Check out my website at www.dksuttonwrites.com.

Join my Facebook reader's group at facebook.-com/groups/cafedk/ We have a lot of fun, and I always post my new stuff there first. You can also sign up for my newsletter to get the latest information.

I also have a Pinterest board for my books. You may have to wade through crochet patterns to get to them, but each board is labeled with the name of the book. They contain photos and other things that inspired me when writing. I'm also on twitter and Instagram.

Please consider leaving a review of Talk to Me on Amazon, Goodreads, Bookbub or wherever you review books. Reviews can really help books show up in Amazon searches so they can then reach more readers.

Thanks again,

DK SUTTON

About the Author

D.K. Sutton loves writing MM romance sprinkled with humor. As an introvert, she has always been a little awkward (and a lot geeky). Turns out, those are handy traits for a writer. Her books are mostly low angst and slow burn. There are always exceptions since her characters don't always play by the rules. She enjoys writing about slightly flawed characters in compromising situations. She has a passion for writing LGBTQ+ stories, because the world needs more love and inclusion and books with queer representation.. For a list of all her books, please turn the page.

For more books and updates sign up for her newsletter here or check out her website at dksuttonwrites.com. You can also visit her reader group at facebook.com/groups/cafedk/

Also By D. K. Sutton

(Not So) University Series

My (Not So) Slutty Professor

My (Not So) Grumpy Professor

My (Not So) Straight Professor

My (Not So) Bossy Professor

Broken Series:

Broken Sidewalks

Trials of Love Series

Trial & Error

The Virgin Pirate

Chasing Santa-A Trials of Love Christmas Novella

Sweet Regrets and Other Holiday Stories

Sloan Brothers Series:

Talk to Me

Equal Opportunity Player-A Sloan Brothers Short

Message Received coming July 2022

Standalones

Accidental Detour

As Addison Lloyd

Y/A LGBT ROMANCE

Dublin High & Westbridge Academy

Reading Order

Merry Little Lies Aaron & Cian

Invincible Me Rob & Caleb

Waiting for Her Carli & Maia

When September Comes Boonie & Dylan

Starr Struck Jade & Mark

Facebook.com/addisonlloydwrites

Pinterest.com/addisonlloyd605

Addison Lloyd on Amazon

Printed in Great Britain
by Amazon

22414648R00111